JACK

VEGAS KINGS BOOK 1

MCKENNA JAMES

JACK

VEGAS KINGS BOOK 1

By Mckenna James

Cover Design by
Moonstruck Cover Design & Photography
moonstruckcoverdesign.com

Startled, I look up as the door bursts open and Ace, one of my best friends, strolls in like he owns the place. Cindy, my assistant, trails behind him, looking flustered.

"I'm sorry. He insisted you'd want to see him—"

"Jack *always* wants to see me," Ace interrupts.

His face breaks into a wide smile as he sinks into the chair opposite me. He winks at Cindy, whose cheeks turn a bright shade of pink—never mind the fact that she's in her fifties and happily married; Ace has an effect of every woman he meets.

"It's fine," I assure Cindy.

It wasn't her fault—I could've barricaded myself into a bulletproof bunker, and Ace would have found a way in. Nothing stops him from getting what he wants. Cindy nods, relieved, and then walks out, closing the door behind her.

"Okay." I shut my laptop and turn my attention to my friend. "What do you want?"

He pretends to be wounded. "Is that any way to greet your closest friend?"

"When you disrupt me while I'm trying to get things organized for a meeting, yes," I grumble, even though I am kind of grateful for the disturbance. "And for the record, when I told Cindy I wasn't to be interrupted, I specifically mentioned *you*," I feel obliged to add.

"Ouch," Ace winces. "I'd take that personally if I wasn't such an easygoing guy." He leans back in his chair and rests his hands behind his head.

"Just get to the damn point, assuming you have one," I say, releasing an exasperated sigh.

"Well, since you asked so nicely." A wicked smirk forms on his lips. "I took the liberty of arranging Asher's bachelor party."

"You mean the one he specifically asked *me* to plan because he didn't want you anywhere near it?" I query.

"That's the one." He nods, looking pretty proud of himself. "I figured I'd do you a favor and take care of everything. I do all the work, and you take credit. How easy is that?"

I groan; nothing is ever easy when Ace is involved.

Ace, Asher, King and I have been friends for years, since elementary school. We'd seen each other through the highest of highs and some really depressing lows, but the thing that stood out was we were all there for each other, no matter what. I joke about Ace and his cheeky attitude getting on my nerves, but the truth is, he's one of the most genuine people I know. My life wouldn't be the same without him in it—although it would probably be a hell of a lot less complicated.

"Are you trying to get me in trouble?" I grumble.

"I have no idea what you're talking about." He gives me an innocent look that might work on someone who doesn't know him as well as I do. "And you get yourself into enough trouble without my help. Take last week, for example. Aren't you just a little bit embarrassed losing a big tournament to an amateur, barely old enough to drink?"

He's referring one of Lake's friends, Mauve, who kicked my

ass during a poker event. She beat me fair and square—not that I'll ever admit that to Ace.

"I let her win," I grumble.

"Yeah, bullshit." Ace chuckles.

"Back to Asher's bachelor party. Are you trying to tell me you really had the spare time to plan a farewell to bachelorhood hurrah worthy of one of our closest friends?"

He's right—I *didn't* have the time, but that's not the point. As tempted as I am to just let Ace run with whatever he has arranged, I know Asher will kill me if he finds out. He left me explicit instructions to not let Ace anywhere near the planning stages of his bachelor night.

My intercom buzzes. I look down and see it's Cindy, so I press answer.

"Sorry to interrupt, but Asher's here," Cindy murmurs. "He said you arranged to see him?"

"I did?" I raise my eyebrows at Ace, who shrugs innocently.

"Don't be so suspicious all the time," Ace drawls, his dark eyes sparkling. "It'll give you an ulcer. I'm trying to help you out, remember?"

I narrow my eyes, knowing full well Ace never does anyone any favors without expecting something in return. Not even for his best friends.

We both look up as the door opens, and Asher swaggers in. His hands are buried deep in the pockets of his Armani suit. With his disheveled hair, five o'clock shadow, and the absence of his usual relaxed smile, he looks stressed—which is to be expected of a guy who's about to marry the love of his life.

Being the romantic that he is, Asher flew Lake to Paris one weekend so he could propose to her at the top of the Eiffel Tower. She of course said yes, and now here we are, six months later, and the big day is just around the corner.

"Okay, so what's the big emergency?" Asher asks. "Lake is

freaking out because I'm missing our rehearsal dinner's rehearsal."

Ace blinks at him. "Is that seriously a thing?"

"When your future wife to-be is as anxious about things going wrong as *mine* is, everything's a thing." Asher's voice is dry. He looks at his watch and sighs. "Seriously, Jack, you've got five minutes and then I'm leaving."

"Five minutes is all he ever needs," Ace promises him.

"Isn't that what women want, a guy who can get the job done fast?" I quip.

"Jack here was just filling me in on what he has planned for your bachelor party," Ace explains to Asher. "You're going to love it. Honestly, I couldn't have organized it better myself."

I cough to smother a laugh. Could he be any more obvious?

"Really?" Asher looks suspiciously from Ace to me. I smile innocently at him. "Why do I feel like something bad is about to happen?"

"It's probably just the fact that you're getting married," Ace deadpans. "Stop worrying so much. Jack has made sure your last hurrah as a single lad will be unforgettable." Asher groans, but Ace ignores his lack of enthusiasm and continues. "Everything is sorted. All you have to do is show up."

"Fine," Asher grumbles, then he directs his gaze to me. "But why is Ace telling me all of this and not you?"

"Jack is trying hard to meet a deadline, and I wanted to make sure he preserves his energy," Ace jumps in before I can open my mouth. Asher looks at me for confirmation, and I shrug, then sit back and enjoy the show. "Besides, you were late," Ace hastily adds. "He's already run through his plans once. Don't make the poor man do it again."

"Yeah, well, you're lucky I made it here at all," Asher mutters, distracted with his phone. "Fine, just tell me when and where, and I'll be there." His shoulders roll forward in defeat. It's like he knows what's really going on but has bigger issues to deal with. "Can I go now?"

"Sure." Ace nods. "We'll see you at eight."

"Hold up, *tonight*?" I snap my head up and glare at Ace.

"What, you didn't realize the party you planned is tonight?" Asher asks, his eyes narrowing at me.

"You know how bad our friend here is with remembering dates," Ace smoothly replies, leaning back in his chair. He flashes me a look. "Right, Jack?"

"Apparently," I murmur, shooting him a death stare.

"You good with tonight?" Ace asks Asher.

Asher shrugs. "Sure. Lake's only stipulation was that it has to be at least two weeks before the wedding. Not that she doesn't trust you guys, or anything like that."

"I wouldn't trust us either." Ace guffaws at his own joke.

Asher glances at his phone again, before muttering something under his breath. He heads for the door, stopping just before he reaches it. He turns around.

"Oh, one more thing." His eyes narrow at Ace. "No strippers."

"Say what?" Ace looks at Asher like he's grown two heads.

"You heard me." Asher speaks firmly, like it isn't up for discussion. "I don't want any strippers. No dancers. No entertainers—nothing."

"So, I should cancel the clown and the bearded lady?" I can't resist asking.

"They're fine, so long as they're appropriately dressed."

I rub my jaw to hide my amusement because I know Ace isn't going to handle this well. For him, the idea of not having strippers at a bachelor party is like having a keg party with no keg.

"B-but it's your bachelor party," Ace sputters in disbelief.

He looks at me for support, but I shake my head. He's on his own with this one. The last time I got between one of Ace and his antics, I came out second best. Ace isn't ready to give up yet, though. He stands up and glares at Asher, fists clenched, like he's ready for a fight.

"What self-respecting man doesn't want strippers at his bachelor party?"

"The kind of man who refuses to disrespect his future wife," Asher replies, his tone calm. "I'm serious, Ace. I'm not interested. Whatever girls you've no doubt already hired for the night, go and *un*-hire them."

"Fine," Ace grumbles, scowling at Asher. "But you really suck the fun out of everything, you know that?"

"Tell you what, when you get married, you can have all the strippers you want," Asher assures him. "I'm going, but I'll see you both tonight."

Asher lets himself out, leaving me alone to deal with a seething Ace. He paces back and forth in front of my desk like his whole existence has been called into question, while I watch in amusement.

"Can you believe that?" Ace rants.

"It's his call," I say with a shrug. "If the dude doesn't want strippers, he doesn't want strippers."

"Oh, he wants them," Ace argues. "He just wants to be able to tell Lake he did everything he could to avoid them being there."

"Yeah, I'm pretty sure that's not right," I say with a smirk. "The guy is pretty smitten with Lake."

"So? That doesn't mean he can't still appreciate the female form. Or at the very least, let *me* appreciate it," Ace whines.

Ace didn't take the news of Asher's impending marriage too well. I know he's happy for our friend, but at the same time, it's always been the four of us, the Vegas Kings. The idea that one of us would give all that up for a chick took a lot for Ace to get used to. Me, on the other hand, I get it. I haven't found the right woman, but I can say without a doubt that I'd happily give up my bachelorhood for her.

"Is there anything you need me to do for tonight?" I ask him, trying to shift the subject.

"No, it's all sorted. I took the liberty of booking out one of the suites at your hotel. Just be there at eight." He glances at his phone and sighs, all the previous excitement he had about the night gone. "Speaking of, I better get going too. I still have a few things to organize."

"I'm sure even without the entertainment, it will be a great night."

"Sure," he mutters, sulking as he stomps over to the door. "As fun as a fucking kids party."

With Ace gone, I get back to finishing the report, ready for the meeting with the board tomorrow. I sit back and rub my neck. I'm feeling the stress today because it's exactly two years since my father died.

Dad and I had a difficult relationship. He expected a lot from me, and no matter how much work I put into the hotel and casino, he'd always remind me that without him, I wouldn't be in the position I was in. Maybe he was right, but that shouldn't take away from the fact that I've worked my ass off to make something of myself.

Since his death, I'd turned The Royal into one of the top hotel gaming casinos in Vegas. Though, Asher would argue that, since he is the owner of my biggest competition, The Grandiose. I sigh because just thinking about my father being at that meeting brings out the anxiety in me.

"Jack?"

I look up to find Cindy peeking into my office.

"Just letting you know I'm heading off."

"Thanks, Cindy. Have a good night."

She hesitates, tucking a strand of gray hair behind her ear. She won't meet my eyes, like there's something on her mind. She pushes the door open and stumbles toward me, placing something on my desk.

"What's this?" I ask, picking it up.

"My resignation," she mumbles, her cheeks glowing red.

"You're leaving me?" I say in surprise.

Cindy has been with me for years. She knows me better than I know myself, and the thought of training someone new makes me feel sick. Not to mention the fact that I don't have the time to go through hundreds of applications to end up with someone who might do 'half' the job Cindy has been spoiling me with since she started.

"I'm so sorry, Jack. You know I love working here, but my mother is ill," she explains. "She's moving in with us so I can become her full-time caregiver."

"I'll be sorry to see you go, but I understand, of course," I murmur, feeling a twinge of sadness. "Thanks, Cindy. I'll see you tomorrow."

She gives me a relived smile and then walks out, closing the door behind her. I sigh and lean back in my chair, the letter still in my hands. I don't open it; I don't need to. It doesn't change the fact that she's leaving. Shutting my laptop with a thud, I push Cindy's resignation out of my mind and call for my driver, Victor, to pick me up. The last thing I want to be is late for the bachelor party I apparently planned.

❦

The doorman greets me as I walk through the front doors of my apartment complex, one of the most exclusive residences in Vegas. The lobby itself is impressive with chandeliers and gold accented fixtures, but it's nothing compared to my penthouse, which occupies the entire top floor. I fell in love with it the moment I saw it, with its modern contemporary design and huge open living areas—probably because it's the complete opposite to the closed off, sterile mansion I grew up in. That place terrified the crap out of me. I was sure it was haunted. Why else would there be so many rooms my father would never let me into?

After he died, I discovered there were many reasons for this, like the fetish collection he had hidden in one room, and the impressive collection of top shelf whiskeys that were worth a small fortune in another, which I can happily say are mine now —the whiskey, that is, not the fetish collection. I gave that to Ace.

I swipe my key in the elevator and press level forty. When the doors open, Cat is sitting there, meowing angrily at being left alone for most of the day. I lean down to pat him as he frantically weaves between my legs.

"Hey, little guy," I murmur.

He follows me through to the kitchen. I walk around the Italian marble counter to the huge walk-in pantry and find his biscuits. I throw some into his bowl, which he wolfs down hungrily. I'd never been an animal person until a few weeks ago —in fact, I *hated* them.

But when I saw Cat hanging out the back of the casino, stealing scraps out of the dumpster when I made the mistake of paying him some attention. He was just a skinny little kitten, and I felt sorry for the guy, so I took him home. He was skittish at first, but after a few nights, he came around. I guess I did too.

The last few days, I've actually found myself looking forward to coming home to him. In some strange way, Cat made me realize how lonely I am sometimes.

Before Cat, I used to spend more time staying in the penthouse of my hotel than here. I told myself it was easier when I was working late, but it was more than that. Sometimes I just craved the interaction I never got at home, even if it was just with the room service attendant or having a drink in the bar. That was another thing my father hated when he was alive. By taking up one of the best rooms, I was taking away from the profit of the hotel. His biggest concern was always profit.

Right through my childhood it was just the three of us: me, my sister, Piper, and Dad. Mom died just after giving birth to Piper, when I was three. My sister struggles with my mom's death to this very day. I think in her mind, she's responsible for Mom's death.

After Mom died, Dad shut us out completely. He left the job of raising us to the nanny, Maria, who was more of a parent to us than Dad ever was. He spent all his time working. Maybe the reason I was upset about Cindy leaving is because she reminds me a lot of Maria. I guess that's another thing I can add to the list of things to discuss with my therapist.

❦

I shower and then get dressed, choosing a dark gray Armani suit and a matching tie, then I take a few moments to style my hair and spray on some cologne. Cat wanders into my room just as I'm fastening my favorite Rolex to my wrist; it's one my grandfather gave to me for my eighteenth birthday.

"You shouldn't be in here."

He ignores me and jumps on my bed and starts washing

himself. I shake my head because the little shit already thinks he owns the place.

"At least wait till I'm gone before you take over my room," I grumble, giving him a scratch behind the ears. He licks his lips in response.

Grabbing my jacket, I shrug it on, slide my wallet into my pocket, and reach for my phone. There's a missed call from Piper, so I call her back, knowing she'll be worried about me because of Dad's anniversary.

"Just making sure you're not drowning in a bath full of alcohol."

"Straight to the point as usual." I grin.

"Is there any other way to be?" She pauses. "You okay?"

"I'm fine. It's just another day, right?"

"Yep." she agrees. "Want some company?"

"I would, but Ace planned this stupid bachelor party for Asher tonight—"

"Hold up, I thought you were supposed to be in charge of that?"

"As if Ace wasn't always going to find a way to organize it," I scoff. "You know what he's like."

"Yeah. Okay, then have a good night. Say hi to the guys for me."

"I will. See you tomorrow."

I feel bad for a moment because I get the feeling Piper's more down over Dad than I am. I contemplate calling Asher and telling him I can't go, but I know while Ash would be fine with it, both Ace and Piper would kill me.

Sliding my phone into my pocket, I take the elevator downstairs and walk outside where Victor is waiting for me. I climb into the back of the car and sigh. Fuck, I'm tired. It's not surprising really, considering how hard I've been working myself lately. It's what I do around the anniversary of Dad's death to keep myself busy. Anything to take my mind off things. I told Piper I was fine, but honestly, I never handle this time of year well.

Maybe I'm harboring more resentment toward my father than I care to admit. The more I think about it, a night of drinking too much with my friends might be exactly what I need. I'm actually looking forward to seeing what Ace has organized.

Nobody plans a party quite like Ace.

CHAPTER TWO

"**L**ook, please, just leave," Mom begs. "This is not the time or the place. It's my husband's funeral, for Christ's sake."

"We appreciate that, and while I feel for you, it doesn't change the fact that we need our money. Either you fix this today, or we'll find a way to make you fix it."

I huddle behind the side wall of the funeral home, my heart pounding as I watch the three big, scary looking men accost my mother. Only one of them speaks. The other two stand back with their fists clenched by their sides, like their main purpose is to instill as much fear into my mom as possible. It's working too. She's trying to remain strong, but I can tell from the look in her eyes she's scared. Hell, *I'm* scared. Mostly because I have no idea who these men are or what they want.

"Please, just leave, before someone sees you," Mom repeats in a hushed tone. "I'll handle it, but not today."

The man in charge stares long and hard at Mom. To her credit, she doesn't waver. She holds his gazes with a strength that challenges his, until he eventually nods.

"Fine," he murmurs. "You have forty-eight hours to settle

your husband's debt, or there will be consequences."

Husband's debt?

I wasn't even aware my father was in debt.

The three men wander off, disappearing into a fancy looking BMW. I watch as it takes off down the street, waiting until it's out of sight before I tentatively approach Mom. Surprise flickers in her eyes as she turns to see me. She forces a smile, but we both know I saw that whole exchange.

"Ellie," she says, her expression uneasy. "What are you doing out here?"

"What's going on?" I demand.

I have so many questions, but I'm not sure I'm ready to hear the answers to them.

"It's nothing, honey. Just some business your father left unattended."

She forces her lips into a thin, transparent smile and tries to guide me back inside, but I stand my ground. I know what I heard. This is more than just some silly little oversight that can be dealt with tomorrow. That man said my father had a debt. A debt that he expected *us* to pay for now Dad is gone. What kind of trouble did my father get himself into?

"Don't worry about it," Mom says, almost begging me to let it go. "Let's go back inside."

"No, I *am* worried about it," I say, determined to get some answers. "What aren't you telling me? What debt were they talking about? Was Dad in trouble?"

I keep pressuring her, and she finally cracks. She covers her face with her hands as the tears flow. I wrap my arms around her, feeling bad that I've upset her. But more than that, I'm worried about how bad the situation is. Losing Dad was hard enough, and since it was suicide, the insurance company refuses to pay out. We're barely keeping ourselves floating as it is. More debts are the last thing we need.

"Mom," I whisper. Now I'm the one who's begging. *"Please* talk to me. I want to help."

"There is no helping," Mom wails. She looks at me, her eyes glassy as a fresh lot of tears fill them. I've never seen her look so scared in my life. "Your father owed a lot of money to a lot of people."

"What kind of people?" I ask, an uneasy feeling forming in my stomach.

"Not very understanding people." She sighs and wipes her eyes, then she pulls me closer for a hug. "I don't know what we're going to do," she weeps.

"It's going to be okay," I soothe her.

She shakes her head. "No, that's the thing. It *won't* be okay, Ellie. Those men…" She takes a deep breath as her voice trembles. "We're not talking about a small amount of money. Your father owed those men hundreds of thousands of dollars."

"What? How?" I whisper.

I feel sick. Was it drugs? No. My father wasn't that kind of man. Or maybe I didn't know him as well as I thought I did.

"Gambling."

My father had a gambling problem.

Mom shakes her head, like she's still coming to terms with it herself.

Suddenly, things start making sense. I couldn't understand how my father could have killed himself without so much as a thought to how it might affect us. He took the easy way out, but he was probably thinking all his problems would disappear. Instead, they've been shifted onto us.

"It's okay, Mom. I promise I will figure this out." On the outside, I'm trying my best to be strong for her, but inside, I feel more scared and alone than I've ever felt. I wrap my arm around her and kiss her on her forehead. "Let's just go back inside."

"But I look like I've been crying," she protests in a hollow voice.

"We're at a funeral, remember?" I remind her with a tiny smile on my face. "That's kind of expected."

She laughs, and I take in as much of my mother's smile as I can; it's something I haven't seen in days. Ever since we came home and found my father lifeless in his car in the garage.

It was a morning I'll never forget. I was late getting ready for college, like always. I remember walking into the kitchen and seeing a fresh pot of coffee brewing, dishes in the sink, the TV playing the morning news in the background. It was just like any other day. I could even hear Dad's car humming in the garage, like it did every morning before he went to work. Only that day, the humming didn't stop.

I knew before I even entered the garage something was wrong. The figure of my father's body slumped over the wheel confirmed it for me.

The rest of the day passes in a blur. My face hurts from smiling, my arms hurt from hugging people who wanted to share their condolences, and if I have to say to one more person that I'm okay, I'm going to snap.

Deep down, I'm not sure we will be okay. Somehow, I'd managed to block those men from my mind, but now, sitting at home, basking in the aftermath of what had to be one of the worst days of my life, it's all I can think about.

Mom's already in bed, even though it's only late afternoon. I'm sure she isn't asleep, but she probably needs time to herself to process everything, so I give her some space. As hard as this has all been for me, I can't even imagine what she must be going through.

My heart broke for her after Dad's death. It came from out of nowhere, completely unexpected. She and Dad were the perfect couple, the kind who did everything together, who still looked at one another the same way they did when they first met thirty years ago. For so long, they had what I wanted. Now, I'm not sure of anything. If my father lied about this, what other things had he been hiding?

I look around, the silence almost unbearable. The walls feel like they're closing in on me. I swallow and stand up, pacing the living room.

I need to get out of here.

I reach down to scoop up my phone. Just as I do, it buzzes with a message.

It's Bea, one of my closest friends.

Bea: Feel up for a coffee?

Me: It's like you can read my mind.

I creep upstairs to my room and get changed. I'm still wearing the black dress I wore to the funeral. I tie my long dark hair back in a loose bun and then go downstairs.

There's light under Mom's door, but I don't want to knock, just in case she's asleep. Instead, I write her a note and leave it on the kitchen counter. With everything that's happened, I don't want her worrying if she wakes up and finds me gone.

Grabbing the keys, I lock up and head out to my car, then I drive toward the diner Bea and I always meet at. The coffee is average, at best, but it's cozy and familiar, which is just what I need right now.

I spot Bea immediately as I walk into the diner. She stands as I walk over to her, and she wraps her arms around me. If anyone understands what I'm going through, it's her. Bea lost her Dad when she was twelve. I was there to help her through it, just like she's helping me through it now.

"How are you holding up?" she asks as we sit.

"Terribly," I admit in a hollow voice.

God, that's the first time I've admitted out loud how much I'm struggling.

Bea nods, reaching out for my hand. "It'll get easier. It doesn't feel like it now, but it will; I promise."

"I'm not sure it *will* get easier," I mumble, fighting back tears. She gives me a quizzical look as I take a breath and summon up the courage to tell her everything. "After the service, I went outside to check on Mom. There were these men hassling her. It turns out my dad owes..." I swallow and correct myself. Telling Bea makes this feel so much more real. "My dad *owed* some bad people a lot of money."

"What do you mean?" Bea asks, looking confused. "To who?"

"A loan shark, I think," I say, not sure what the correct terminology for these men is. My hands fidget on the table in front of me.

"Are you serious? *Your* dad owed money to a loan shark?"

Bea starts laughing, but it's not out of disrespect; it's because the idea of my dad associating with anyone like that sounds ridiculous. My father was a typical, middle-class American Dad with the family, a normal job, a normal life. He was happy. *We* were happy. At least that's what everyone thought. Including me.

"Ellie, what are you talking about?"

"He had gambling debts," I whisper.

"Are you serious?" Her eyes widen even more. "Like how much are we talking?"

"Two hundred thousand," I whisper, my throat constricting.

"Two hundred thousand *dollars?*" Bea screeches.

"You want to yell it a little louder?" I hiss, turning around to make sure nobody overheard her. "I'm sure there are people outside who didn't quite hear you."

"I'm sorry," she whispers, her eyes wide. "It's just that's so much more than I expected you to say. He obviously wasn't very good at it."

"That's beside the point," I grumble.

"I know. I'm sorry." She regains her composure before continuing. "Okay, so he owed them money, but he can't pay it," Bea states the obvious. "Surely that's the end of it?"

"Apparently not." I shake my head. "These guys don't care that my father is dead. They want their cash, and now that he has passed, it's on us."

"But that's not fair," Bea argues, her dark eyes flashing. "Can't you do something, like go to the cops?"

"I get the feeling that wouldn't be a good idea," I mutter.

Going to the police will only make the situation worse. The only way to make this go away is by coming up with two hundred grand and fast. The problem is, we don't have access to that kind of money. Heck, I don't even have a job.

"What are you going to do?" Bea asks.

"I need to work out a plan," I say, trying to convince myself as much as her. "Maybe if I get a job, I can work out a way to pay it off."

"These dudes don't sound like the kind of guys who'll accept a twenty-year payment plan," Bea points out.

"What else am I going to do?" I ask her in a shrill voice.

I take in a deep breath, holding back the tears that are threatening to erupt; I know she's right. A job isn't going to solve this, but maybe if I can show them I'm trying to find a solution, it will buy me some time. At least until I can figure out what my real move is.

I swallow a laugh. My real move? I have no moves. There is no way out of this mess. These guys aren't going to listen to reason, and they're certainly not going to listen to me. And it's not like I can pay the money back myself.

"If we don't come up with the money, I'm worried they'll do something to Mom."

"Or you." Bea frowns.

I nod, but I don't care about me. I just want to know Mom is safe.

"It's going to be okay. I promise." Bea puts her hand over mine and gives me a reassuring smile. "Maybe I can help."

"Help me? How?" I ask.

"I have a friend whose sister does some work that pays well," she begins. "I can—"

"Thanks, but I'll pass," I cut her off. "Anything that pays that well isn't going to be something I'm cut out for."

"No, this is all above board," she assures me. "These are just *very* high-class rich clients. And it isn't stripping or anything like that. It's just dancing—"

"Dancing?" I repeat with a laugh. "Have you seen me dance?"

"All I'm saying is let me pass on your number. If you sit down with her, she might be able to work something out with you that you'll feel comfortable with," she suggests.

"Okay, sure" I agree, realizing how desperate the situation is. I need to at least consider something that would allow me to pay this off faster. "Give her my number."

"Great," Bea says. "So aside from that, how are you really? That funeral was so sad."

"It was hard." I shake my head, still overwhelmed by every-thing that happened over the last week. "I'm coping, but I'm really worried about Mom. Dad's debts are a whole new level of stress she didn't need. We were in pretty bad financial shape before all of this. She knew she was probably going to have to sell the house and everything else we owns, and now this..." I sigh and rub my temples. "I'm worried this will push her over the edge."

"Your mom will be okay. She's strong, Ellie. Just like you are," Bea assures me.

I smile at my friend, wishing I felt as convinced.

"I better get home," I say, getting to my feet. "I'm nervous leaving her alone for too long, given the circumstances."

"Okay, call me if you need anything. Promise?"

I smile and hug my friend. "Promise."

$\clubsuit$

*B*ack at home, my note still sits on the kitchen counter, untouched, which probably means Mom hasn't left the bedroom. I crumble it up and toss it in the trash, then head up to my room. Her light still shines under the door. I stand still for a second, listening for any sign that she's awake, but silence greets me.

I walk to my room, closing the door behind me then get straight into bed, still dressed. Switching off the lamp, I lie there in the darkness, a ball of nerves eating away at my stomach. It's just past seven in the evening, but all I want to do is go to sleep and forget. The problem is, I can't stop my brain from ticking over. I'm not even sure I'm tired enough to sleep, but I figure if I lay here long enough, it will have to come eventually.

"Ellie?"

I roll over as Mom pokes her head into my room. I flick the lamp on and push the blankets back, sitting up as she walks over and joins me on the edge of the bed.

"Are you okay?" I ask, placing my hand over hers.

She smiles at me. "I came in here to ask you the same thing."

"I'm fine," I assure her.

"You're in bed, still dressed at seven in the evening," she points out.

"So were you," I remind her with a smile.

"I at least had my light on," she replies, a small smile on her lips. "How are you holding up?"

"I'm okay." I shrug.

I feel like that's all I ever say these days. I'm fine. I'm okay. I'm not, but I can't tell Mom that. She has enough to worry about. She hesitates and reaches for my hand, like she has something else she wants to talk to me about. I brace myself; there isn't much more I can handle today.

"Ellie, what you heard at the funeral, it isn't something I want you worrying about."

"Of course I'm worried about it," I tell her.

"Well, don't be." Her voice is firm. "I'm going to take care of it."

"How?" I challenge her. "Mom, you can't fix this alone, and you shouldn't have to—"

"Ellie, please," Mom sighs. "Just stay out of it. Promise me you'll leave it for me to handle?"

I stare at her for a moment and then nod. "Fine. I'll stay out of it."

She leans over and kisses me on the forehead and then stands up.

"I have to get ready for work."

"You're working tonight?" I ask, worried.

Mom is a nurse at the Summerlin Hospital Medical Center. She worked hard all her life, but now with Dad gone, I knew she was probably going to have to work even harder just to keep us afloat. I didn't think that would begin the same day we buried Dad.

Mom nods. "I've picked up a few extra shifts this week to try to..." Her voice trails off. "There's plenty of food in the fridge. Call me if you need me, okay?"

She walks out, quietly closing the door behind her.

As soon as I hear the hum of her car taking off down the

street, I stand up. How can she expect me to sit back and not to do anything? Of course I'm going to try to help her fix this mess. There's no way she can raise the kind of cash we need by picking up a few extra shifts.

I trudge downstairs and open the fridge. Mum wasn't kidding. It's packed full of casseroles and cakes and other things that neighbors and friends made for us in the days following Dad's death. I guess that's what happens when people don't know what to say or do following a tragedy like this; they cook.

I pull out a chicken pie and cut myself a slice. I don't bother heating it. I'm not that hungry anyway. Sitting at the table with a fork, I stab at it while trying to come up with a plan. I'll feel better if I have something worked out, just in case we need it.

My phone rings on the table, making me jump. The fork falls from my hands, the sound of it hitting the tiles almost enough to make me pass out. Still shaking, I pick up my phone and stare at the unknown number flashing on the screen. My heart races... What if it's them? I shake off the thought because they don't seem like the type of thugs to follow things up with a phone call. Turning up to make threats in person is much more their style.

I hold my breath and press answer.

"Hello?"

"Ellie? Hey, girl. This is Candy. Bea's friend? She told my you were looking for a job. I've had a girl cancel on me, if you're interested in working a bachelor party?"

My first instinct is to say no, but I can't force the words out. Probably because I know this might just be our only option. Besides, Bea said it isn't stripping—it's dancing. Sure, I'm not the best dancer in the world, but it's for a bachelor party. The guys will probably be too drunk and high on drugs to notice my lack of dancing skills. I close my eyes, barely able to believe what I'm about to say.

"Sounds great," I chirp, my heart in my throat. "Just tell me where and when."

"Can you be at The Royale Hotel in an hour? I'll give you a bonus because of the short notice."

My heart races. Tonight? I thought I'd have more time to psych myself up. I flex my fingers, my hands suddenly very sweaty, and then I swallow.

"Sure. I'll be there."

"Great." She sounds relieved. "I'll leave your details with reception. It's on the top floor. It's the only room on the level; you can't miss it."

"Great. Thanks," I manage to say.

I hang up and stare at the pie in front of me. I'm working a bachelor party at the penthouse of one of the most exclusive hotels in Vegas.

Oh God.

Please don't let me regret this.

❧

*A*n hour doesn't give me long to get ready, so I race upstairs and rifle through my closet, quickly realizing how totally unprepared I am for this job. Nothing I own is suitable for this at all. Grabbing my phone, I call Bea in a panic.

"What's wrong?" she asks when she hears me sobbing.

"Candy called and asked me to work a party tonight, and now I have nothing to wear."

"Calm down. I have just the thing," Bea soothes. "Go do your hair and make-up, and I'll be there in five."

I'm like a zombie as I do my hair and make-up. I leave my dark hair down so falls in layers around my face and shoulders. I go heavier than I usually would with my make-up, but not so much that I look like a hooker.

Why not? It's just one step below exotic dancing.

The pit in my stomach is growing bigger by the second. I'm not sure I can do this, but I'll kick myself if I don't at least try. Who knows, maybe I'll surprise myself. All I have to do is walk in there, smile, and dance around for a group of drunken idiots, and I'll get paid. Easy. At least, for anyone else it would be easy.

For me?

There's no way I can do this. I'm just about to call Candy and cancel, when Bea pounds on the front door. She gives my hair and make-up an appreciative nod when I open the door.

"Nice," she says. "Now hurry up and put this on."

"I don't think I can do this," I whisper.

"Why not go there and try?" Bea coaxes. "I think you'll regret it if you don't."

She's right. I know she's right. I nod and motion for her to hand me the dress she's clutching—at least I think that's what the tiny scrap of fabric is. It looks about two sizes too small for me and way too short, but I guess that's the whole point. Slipping my robe off, I pull the dress on, then throw the short white jacket she hands me over the top.

"The damn jacket is longer than the dress," I growl.

"You look sexy as hell... Oh no, girl." Bea looks down at my feet and shakes her head.

"You're lucky I know you so well," she mutters. She reaches into her bag like Mary-freaking-Poppins and pulls out a pair of heels so high they might be stilts.

"You want me to break my neck, don't you?" I mutter, slipping them on.

"If that's what you have to do, then deal with it. Now go," she says, pushing me out the door. "And call me when you're done!"

CHAPTER THREE

"Where the hell are you?"

Ace's voice barks down the line, but I can barely hear him over the beat of the music pumping in the background. I shake my head. I'm only a few minutes late. He's probably worried that Asher will figure out he organized the whole thing, as if he doesn't already know.

"Relax, I'm stepping into the elevator now," I assure him. "I'll be there in a few."

I end the call and slide my phone into my pocket. The doors fling open, and I step inside and hit the top floor.

"Wait, please!" a feminine voice calls out as the doors begin to close.

I put my hand out, triggering the sensor, and they burst open to reveal a woman standing there. She isn't just any woman, though. With long dark hair that hangs loosely around her shoulders and impossibly long legs that spill out from beneath the short white jacket she's wearing, she's quite possibly the most stunning woman I've ever seen. Her icy blue eyes flicker up and meet mine as she steps into the elevator.

"Thanks," she murmurs, giving me a tight smile.

"What floor?" I ask.

"Top," she replies, avoiding any further eye contact.

Amused, I press the button for the top floor again. That can only mean one thing—Ace ignored Asher's request about the strippers. No doubt he'll try to pin it on me.

"*Fuck.* I can't do this."

I glance at the woman in surprise. I'm no expert when it comes to female emotions and shit, but she looks like she's about to either burst into tears or start punching the elevator wall. Either way, something is obviously bothering her.

"Are you okay?" I ask.

Her head snaps up, and she looks at me like she forgot I was there. A faint glow of pink spreads across her cheeks as she quickly nods, then shakes her head.

"This is *so* not me," she mutters, releasing a harsh laugh. "I tried, but I can't do it."

"Do you want to talk about it?" I offer. "I can be a pretty good listener."

That part is a lie. Piper's always telling me I can't listen for shit, but honestly, I'm not sure what else to say to this girl.

"What the hell is talking going to do?" she snaps. "I'm sorry, I just..." She sighs. "No. There's no way I'll be able to go through with this."

"Then don't."

If she is part of the entertainment that Ace hired—though she really doesn't strike me as the type—I'm worried someone is making her do something she doesn't want to do.

"It's not that simple." She mumbles so softly that I'm pretty sure she didn't mean for me to hear it. "I need the money."

"There are other ways to make money."

"Only a rich person would say that with such ignorance," she replies, her lips twitching.

Burn.

But at least I got her to almost smile. Stepping forward, I press the button for the next floor, holding the doors open when it stops. She looks up in surprise.

"Maybe you should go figure out what's going on in your head," I suggest. "Make sure what you're about to do is for the right reasons."

She's about to argue with me, but then her lips flatten into a thin smile. The sadness in her eyes is impossible to ignore as she gives me a small nod then steps out.

I wait until she's disappeared out of my sight, before I press the button again. The doors start closing, but then just as quickly, they spring open and she's standing there again. I lift my eyebrows in confusion. This woman is so back and forth, and I'm starting to feel dizzy.

"I'm sorry," she blurts out, stepping inside. "I know you think I'm crazy, but I have to do this."

"It's your call," I say with a shrug.

Facing the doors, she fixates her attention on the numbers above as they slowly rise. I stand back, my hands wedged in my pockets. She's made it pretty clear she isn't interested in having a conversation with me. The second the doors open on the top floor, she leaps out. I hang back for a second, and then I follow her across the hallway.

She turns around and eyes me suspiciously. "Are you following me? I said I was fine."

"No." I flash her a smile. "It just looks like we're just headed to the same place."

Her mouth falls open as I step around her and open the door. Ace looks up as I walk inside. He salutes me, and I shake my head.

The party has been going less than ten minutes, and he's already drunk.

"Jack," he drawls as I make my way over to him. He nods

appreciatively at my mystery girl, who is still standing in the doorway, her expression unreadable. "And I thought *I* was the one we had to worry about canoodling with the entertainment," he murmurs.

He gives me a hard slap on the back before strolling over to the door to greet her.

"You must be our missing dancer."

He places his arm around her and motions for her to come inside, but she stands there, staring at him in shock. Her gaze shifts to me, the panic in her eyes catching me off guard. The uneasy feeling from earlier returns, and I'm sure she doesn't belong here.

She's practically begging me for a way out, so I give her one.

"Actually," I say to Ace. "That's my new assistant."

"Your assistant?" Ace's eyebrows shoot up. He stares at me like he's not sure whether to believe me or not. "Since when do assistants dress so hot? And what happened to Cindy?"

"She quit," I explain, ignoring his first question. I don't have an answer for it. "So I'm trialing this one." Fuck, I wish I'd caught her name in the elevator because I'm sure that's going to be Ace's next question. "I'm so short on time at the moment I told her to come with me tonight so she could check out the hotel," I ramble on.

"You invited your new assistant to a bachelor party?" Ace narrows his eyes. "What did you say her name is?"

Fuck.

"Ellie."

We both look at her in surprise when she speaks. She extends her hand to Ace and gives him a tight smile when he takes it, then she turns to me.

"Was there anything else you needed or am I free to go now?"

I wince. At least her icy tone matches the death stare she's giving me.

"I think we're good." I give a firm nod. "I'll walk you out."

She follows me out into the hallway without saying a word. I'm expecting a little gratitude for saving her ass in there, but as soon as the door closes and we're alone, she explodes.

"I can't believe you just did that," she hisses, her eyes flashing.

"Are you serious?" I'm shocked, amused, and a little turned on by her outburst because this girl's got fire. "You were practically begging me for an out, so I gave you one."

"I wasn't begging you for anything," she snaps. "I panicked, but before I had a chance to recover, you swooped in like some kind of hero to save me."

"Because I thought that's what you wanted me to do," I say with laugh, which only makes her more aggravated.

"Well, it wasn't, and now you've gone and told everyone I'm your assistant..." She takes a deep breath, then releases it before continuing. "I can't exactly walk back in there and do the job I was supposed to be getting paid to do now, can I?"

"Excuse me for saying, but it really didn't seem like you wanted to do the job in the first place," I point out.

"Oh, because you know me so well you think you're in the position to make that assumption?" She crosses her arms and glares at me.

"No, that's not what I..."

I sigh and reel myself in. All I seem to be doing is digging myself into a deeper hole.

"Look, I'm sorry if I did something in there that you didn't want me to do. I really was just trying to help you out."

"Yeah, well, you didn't," she grumbles.

I dig through my pockets, pull out my card, and hand it to her.

"What's this?" she asks, reluctantly taking it from me.

"My card," I explain. "I wasn't lying when I said my assistant quit on me. She handed in her resignation this evening."

"I bet she did," she grumbles. "Probably because of all the sexual harassment."

"Cindy," I reply with a smirk. Ellie looks at me quizzically. "That's my assistant's name. She's fifty-three and married with three beautiful kids and a lovely husband. She was with me for nearly five years, and the only reason she's leaving me is because her mother is sick. And since we're being so honest with each other, I wish she wasn't because I'm going to miss the fuck out of her."

Ellie looks down, fingering the edges of my business card. She's clearly embarrassed, which wasn't my intention.

"Look," I add softly. "If you don't want the job, that's fine, but don't have a go at me for pretending to know who you are, but then turn around and do the exact same thing to me."

"I was doing that, wasn't I?" She stares at me, her lips twisting into a frown. "I'm sorry." The sadness is back in her eyes, only this time it's stronger. I can almost feel it. "I guess I'm just not used to people being nice to me for no reason." She studies me for a second. "Speaking of which, why *are* you being so nice?"

"Because you look like you could use a break," I say with a shrug. "I don't know what your situation is, or what's going on in your life, but I think it takes a great deal of courage to even consider doing what you were going to do tonight." She looks at me like she's not sure whether to believe me or not, so I continue. "You don't look like the type of girl who makes a habit out of doing this."

"And you'd know, because you have experience with that *type* of girl?" Her eyes narrow.

Ouch. "I guess I walked into that one."

I swear I see another smile tug at those sexy lips, but then it's gone.

I nod at my card, which she's still holding onto.

"Come in tomorrow at nine a.m., and we'll talk."

"What exactly is it that do you do?" she asks suspiciously, fanning my card in front of her.

Okay, now I'm really shocked.

Being a local celebrity, it isn't too often I meet a woman who doesn't know who I am. I thought her cold attitude toward me was *because* of who I was. My name's right there on the card she's staring at. I should probably tell her that I own the biggest casino and hotel in Vegas—the very same hotel we're standing in, but something stops me.

I don't want to scare her off.

It isn't like I'm *lying* to her by withholding that little bit of information. Right?

"You want to know what I do?" I give her a smile. "Come in and find out."

She stares at me for a moment, her lips pursed tightly together.

"I better get out of here," she murmurs.

She turns around and stalks down the hallway, in the direction of the elevators. I wait until she's out of sight, before I go back in to join the party. The guys exchange a knowing smile when they see me, and I groan, pretty sure I don't want to know what they've been saying behind my back.

"So, new assistant, huh?" King grins and wiggles his eyebrows. "She's pretty fucking hot, dude."

"Yeah, but what happened to Cindy?" Ace grumbles. "I loved her, man."

"I told you. She quit," I grunt.

At least that part's true.

"And you found a replacement already?" Asher, chimes in. His eyes narrow as he gives me a skeptical look. Out of all my friends, he's the one who's likely to keep pushing this until I tell them the truth. "I didn't see her there today when we stopped by."

"She started later, and what can I say? I can work fast when I want to," I reply with a wink. "I mean, did you see those legs?"

Asher and King laugh, while Ace lets out a low whistle.

The guys wouldn't doubt for a second that I'd hired some piece of ass because she looked cute in a short skirt. I'm Jack Stapleton, for God's sake. I'm with a different woman every week. The only way to stop the guys from asking more questions is to make them believe I want to sleep with her. I'm just glad Ellie isn't around to hear me talking about her like that.

"Just be careful mixing business with pleasure." King shakes his head. "Those sexual harassment lawsuits will cost you a fucking fortune."

"You sound like you're speaking from experience," I say with a sly smile.

He waves his hand. "That's a story for another night. But if you want my opinion, Ellie didn't seem that into you."

"She seemed much more into me," Ace agrees.

"Not yet." I ignore Ace and address King. "But once she gets to know me, she won't be able to resist. You know how charming I can be."

The guys laugh, and the conversation moves onto King's next show, coming up in a few weeks, but my mind is still stuck on what he said. She really didn't seem that into me even before I intervened, which is unusual. Still, I have no doubt she'll show up tomorrow for an interview, and after a little consideration, she'll realize I'm offering her a valuable opportunity.

❦

y midnight, I'm feeling pretty wasted, and the longer party drags on, the less I'm able to function. I have to admit, letting loose and enjoying myself is just what I needed. I'm not the only one who's having fun either. Asher seems to be having a blast. He wanders over to me and throws his arm around my shoulders, embracing me in a hug. I laugh because drunk Asher can be a very emotional person.

"I'd like to credit you for organizing such a great night, but I think we all know it wasn't you who planned this." He turns to Ace, who's looking pretty proud of himself. "Thanks, man. I should've trusted you, even if you didn't listen to me about the strippers."

"Aw, shucks, you're gonna make me cry. Come here, man." Ace throws his arm around his friend. "I just hope you know what you're getting yourself into. Personally? I'm never getting married. No fucking way."

"Trust me." Asher chuckles. "When you meet the right girl, you might change your mind."

"I'm on Ace's side with this one," King announces. "And I think we all know Jack will never settle down."

Despite what the guys think, I am open to meeting the right girl and settling down. Having someone to share things with and talk through your highs and lows sounds like a pretty special deal. Maybe it's the alcohol talking, but to me, it sounds down-right amazing.

My thoughts unconsciously drift to Ellie. I love that she stood up for herself, like she didn't care who I was. There was something about her that caught my attention, and it makes me want to learn more about her.

Is she the one? Maybe. Maybe not.

But I'm going to try my hardest to find out.

Who the hell does he think he is?

The way he swooped in to save me like I was some kind of helpless damsel in distress is so chauvinistic. Sure, I froze, but it was only because I was getting my head around what I was about to do; *not* because I needed rescuing. I didn't ask for his help, nor did I want it.

And then, to top it all off, he actually had the nerve to offer me a job? I can only imagine what *that* role will entail. I pull out his business card and snort; who the hell just has their name and number on a business card, with no mention of what they do?

Apparently Jack Stapleton does.

I toss the card into the first trash can I pass without even slowing down. Sorry, Jack, but you can find someone else to kiss your ass—or whatever fetish it is that you're into.

Stomping out of the hotel, I head down the street to where my car is parked. I was too embarrassed to park it any closer to the big, fancy hotel because there's no getting around it—my car is a shit box. But hey, at least it's a reliable shit box that hasn't let me down yet.

I unlock the car and climb in, closing the door with a bang, then I slam my hands against the steering wheel.

"Fuck," I hiss.

There's no other way to look at it; I just lost my only real chance to make some decent money. Not only that, I managed to embarrass myself in front of the hottest guy I've ever laid eyes on. God, I hate that I found him so attractive. Standing in that elevator with him was pure torture. I could feel his eyes on me. God only knows what he was thinking. Probably that I was high on drugs.

Fumbling through my pocket, I grab my phone and call Bea. I need some sympathy, and she's the only person who will understand. She answers on the first ring.

"You didn't go, did you?"

"I went," I defend myself. "I was only there for ten seconds, but it still counts."

"Oh fuck, what happened?" she asks.

I take a deep breath and try to compose myself, but all I want to do is burst into tears. I'm so annoyed at myself for not being able to go through with it. And as much as I want to blame Jack for ruining things for me, deep down I know that if he hadn't have done what he did, I probably would've run out of there anyway.

"Ellie?" Bea prods, her voice softer.

"Yeah, I'm here," I hiccup, trying to calm myself. I close my eyes and focus on my breathing. "It was awful, Bea. Horrible. The worst experience of my life. I shouldn't have gone. I *knew* I wasn't cut out for that kind of thing—"

"I'm sorry I pushed you into it," Bea mumbles.

"Don't be. You were right. I probably would've regretted it if I hadn't have gone. I guess that's the beauty of hindsight, huh?"

"Was it that bad?" Bea sounds sympathetic.

"It was worse. I was a hot mess," I moan. "And then when I saw the sexy guy from the elevator—"

"Wait, I'm confused," she cuts in. "What sexy guy are we talking about?"

"Okay." I take a deep breath. "So I was running late, and the elevator doors were closing. I called out for someone to hold it. As soon as they opened, I wished I hadn't because the guy standing there was so freaking hot."

I groan and cover my face with my hands, aware I'm barely making sense. Even thinking about it makes me cringe. He probably thought I was on drugs or something, with the way I was talking to myself.

"It doesn't sound so bad yet." Bea tries to make me feel better.

"I was a mess," I groan, cringing just thinking about it. "I was talking to myself and freaking out. I was in such a state that he actually *stopped* on another floor and suggested I take a moment to clear my head."

"Aww, he sounds nice," Bea replies.

"Nice?" I grumble. "He wasn't *nice.* Nice would've been informing me we were going to the same place before he followed me into the penthouse."

"Maybe he didn't know?" she offers.

"He pressed the button for me in the elevator. There was only one suite on the entire side of the floor. He knew."

"Well, at least you made it in there," Bea offers. She's trying to cheer me up, but it's not working.

"Yes," I say brightly. "Wonderful. I made it all the way in there, only to go into panic mode and literally freeze on the spot. It was *horrible*, Bea."

"So you ran out?" Bea guesses, her voice full of sympathy.

"Worse," I say. "The hot guy from the elevator thought he'd be a hero and come to my rescue."

"How?"

Bea's voice comes out a few notches higher than normal, and I know she's trying not to laugh. I scowl; this is anything but funny.

"By telling everyone I'm his new assistant." I sigh. "I went along with it and then left. He followed me into the hallway, and I blew up on him."

"You yelled at the poor guy for helping you?" Bea loses her composure and bursts into hysterical laughter. "Oh, boy. I wish I could've been a fly on that wall."

"I can't believe you're taking his side," I whine, not seeing the funny side to this.

"I'm not," Bea protests. "It just sounds like he was genuinely trying to help you."

"Well, I didn't ask for his help," I snap. "And then he had the nerve to suggest I work for him—"

"Back up... He offered you a job?" Bea chortles. "That's so sweet! Does this guy have a name?"

"Jack something." I reach into my pocket, but then remember I threw his card out. "Jack Stapleton," I suddenly recall.

"*Jack Stapleton?*" Bea gurgles.

"Do you know him?" I frown.

"Not personally," she quickly replies. "I think my friend might have mentioned him; I'm not sure. Tall, dark hair, and really hot?"

"You just described most of Vegas' social scene," I snort. "But yeah, it sounds like him."

"So when do you start your new job with your sexy boss?" Bea teases.

"Never. I'm not accepting it," I say firmly. "If he was willing to offer me a job based on what he saw of me tonight, then it's probably something I have zero interest in being a part of."

"Or he could just be a nice guy who wants to help you out?" Bea counters. "I think you should call him at least and hear him out."

"Fine, I'll think about it," I say, if only to end this conversation.

"Make sure you do," Bea says. "Hey, are we still on for breakfast tomorrow?" she adds. "We can postpone if you're not up for it."

"No, I think I need the distraction," I admit. "Usual time?"

"See you then. Call me if you need anything."

"Thanks, Bea."

My heart races as I pull into the driveway. The dark, empty house looks less than inviting. I wish I had the foresight to leave some lights on, especially since I have no idea if we're being watched.

I shiver at the thought.

I'm tempted to drive over to Bea's and spend the night there, but I don't want Mom arriving home at five in the morning and facing the same situation, so I stop the car and force myself to get out. I'm sure that once I'm inside and the house is lit up, I'll feel much better.

Locking the car, I run up the path to the front door. My hands shake as I unlock it. I practically fall inside, closing the door behind me with a thud. I lock both locks and switch on the light. My anxiety eases slightly, but I won't be able to rest until I know the house is empty, so I pick up the baseball bat resting near the front door and quietly check each room.

Satisfied that I'm alone, I make myself a cup of tea and settle down on the couch. There's no way I can go to sleep, so I turn on an old movie and curl up with a blanket. I haven't been able to sleep without some ambient noise since Dad died. In fact, I haven't slept much at all since that night.

My eyes stay focused on the screen in front of me, but I'm not taking much in. I'm so tired I can barely keep awake, but I fight to keep my eyes from closing, until I can't anymore...

"*E*llie?"

I jump, still gripping hold of the bat, but it's swiftly taken out of my hands. It takes a few seconds for my eyes to register that it's Mom standing in front of me. She looks like she doesn't know whether to laugh or cry.

"We're coping well, I see."

"I was being careful, and I guess I fell asleep on the couch," I grumble, struggling to sit up. I wince and rub my neck, which is cramped from sleeping on an odd angle. "If those men were fine with crashing a funeral, I don't think home visits are off limits."

"I told you I'd take care of it," Mom says, sitting on the couch next to me.

"I know, but that doesn't mean I shouldn't be wary in the meantime." I lean over and give her a hug. "It's not only that. It's being here alone after..."

My voice trails off. Mom smiles, her eyes shining with tears.

"I know. It'll get easier," she promises.

"You sound like Bea," I murmur. "Speaking of, I'm supposed to go meet her for breakfast, but I can cancel—"

"Go," Mom orders. "It will do you good to get out of the house and have some fun. Promise me you're not going to worry about the money?" she adds.

"I promise," I say.

At this point, I'm hardly in the position to help anyway.

he next morning, I walk inside our favorite diner and immediately spot Bea, sitting at a table near the back. She looks up and grins at me as I walk over to her, slumping down into the chair. I still can't think about last night without feeling sick, and I'm still no closer to fixing my father's debt problem.

"You're going to that interview," Bea announces as I reach for the menu.

"Good morning to you too," I say, taking a sip of the coffee she's already ordered for me. "And no. I'm not."

"Come on, Ellie," she whines. "Give the guy a chance. See what he's offering before you shut him down. Maybe it pays really well."

"If I knew this was going to be an interrogation, I would've stayed at home," I retort.

Bea sighs. "Just answer me this, and I'll shut up; why did you yell at him when you were probably seconds away from bolting out of there anyway?"

Her question catches me off guard. Bea lifts her eyebrows as she waits for me to reply.

I sigh. "Fine. I was angry at myself because I couldn't go through with it, and I *may* have taken it out on him."

"Then isn't that all the more reason to go in and see him, so you can apologize?"

"No, it's all the more reason to *not* go because he probably thinks I'm crazy," I retort, mimicking her tone. "The only place I'm *going* is back home if you don't drop this, okay?"

"Okay, I'm sorry," Bea sighs. "I'm just trying to help. I know how much this thing with your dad is stressing you out."

"I know you're trying to help, and I appreciate it," I tell her. "But I can't go to that interview, Bea, so *please* stop pushing it."

"Okay, I'll never mention it again," she promises, reaching across the table for my hand. "Hey, if you want, I could hook you up with a few shifts at the club. Just behind the bar with me," she hastily adds when she sees my expression.

Bea works the bar at a high-class men's establishment on the strip called Valentino's. I open my mouth to say no, but I stop myself. Working with Bea is something I can actually handle. Besides, having something to do might help take my mind off the mess that is my life, and every little bit of cash we can get together is going to help.

"I wish you'd offered me that in the first place," I joke.

"You needed real cash, and trust me, the club pays *nowhere* near what last night would have paid."

I feel a pang of guilt. Last night really was my best chance at being able to come to some sort of arrangement with these guys. What if they do something to Mom because we can't come up with the money? I'll never forgive myself.

"I'll speak to my boss later today and see if I can arrange a couple of shifts for you," Bea continues, her voice jolting me back to reality.

"Thanks, Bea." I lean over and kiss her on the cheek. "I'm sorry if I'm snappy; I really do appreciate your help. I'm just so stressed out."

"I get it." She smiles at me. "You just make sure you look after yourself, okay?"

"I will."

❧

*A*fter we finish breakfast, I head home. The whole drive, I can't get what Bea said out of my head. Maybe I should go in there and hear him out and then decide what to do.

It might turn out to be a great opportunity, and he did seem nice. The problem is, I'll never be able to look at him without remembering what a mess I was. I'm sure he only offered me a job because he felt sorry for me.

He's probably forgotten about it, anyway.

CHAPTER FIVE

I tap my pen against my desk in a continuous rhythm, like I do when I'm nervous—

Wait, why the hell am I so nervous?

She's just a woman, like the rest of them.

But that's the thing—she isn't like the rest of them. I don't know why, but in the whole five minutes I'd spent with tell Ellie, I could tell she was different, and I'm excited about the idea of her working with me. Getting to look at those long, slender legs all day will be an added bonus.

With a growl, I toss the pen across the room and watch it bounce off the wall near the door.

"Get it together, man," I mutter, leaning back in my chair.

I glance at the clock again. She's late, which is a bad sign for an assistant, but I'm willing to let it slide, considering we met under strange circumstances. She better have a good reason for running late, though, or I'll have to take her over my knee.

Jesus, Jack. Compose yourself.

I sit there and wait.

And wait.

After an hour passes, I begin to think that maybe she's not coming.

Well, shit.

She actually stood *me* up. I can honestly say with one hundred percent certainty that has never happened to me before. A knock on the door sends a thrill of excitement through me, but it's only Cindy. I try to hide my disappointment as she walks over to me and places a stack of papers on my desk.

"I have some applications for you to look through," she explains. "I've vetted the top ten. There's plenty more if you need them."

The job was only posted yesterday, and more than two hundred people have applied. I'm sure they were all well-qualified for the role, but I wanted none of them.

"Thanks," I mutter sullenly.

"You don't sound excited about the idea."

"Because I'm not."

I'm pouting, and I don't even care. If there's one thing I hate more than anything else, it's interviewing and training people, especially when that person has to work so closely with me. That's why I wanted Ellie to accept the job, to save me the hassle of finding someone. At least I knew I could stand being around her. An even better solution would be for Cindy to stay, but that's not an option.

"You'll figure it out," Cindy assures me, giving me a motherly pat on the back.

She walks out, and I leaf through the applications, feeling about as underwhelmed as I expected to. Experience, diplomas, degrees, everything is there. Any one of them could do a magnificent job, but that's the problem. They're all so *common*. I don't want generic cardboard cut-out. I want someone with a little spark. Someone who'll give me as much shit as I'll probably give them. Someone I'll be looking forward to seeing every morning.

Someone like Ellie.

I run my hands through my hair. God, why can't I stop thinking about her? I know nothing about her, yet she's all I've been able to think about today. And the way she went off on me in the hallway and now not showing up for her interview?

I swallow. I'm starting to think her standing me up is a good thing because if she *were* working here, I'd get nothing done.

⁂

I do my best to buckle down and get some work done, because the business isn't going to run itself, but I'm easily distracted, and it doesn't take long before my mind slips back to Ellie. I start thinking of ways to find her, but it's hard, considering I don't know her last name or anything else about her. Hell, I'm not even sure Ellie is her real name.

But Ace might know.

Picking up my phone, I scroll though my contacts until I find his name.

"I was wondering when I'd hear from you," Ace drawls when he answers. "Hell of a party, huh?"

"You outdid yourself," I agree with a chuckle. "I don't remember half of it."

"Me neither," he admits. "I could do with not seeing a bottle of alcohol for a while, though. My fucking head is killing me."

"Until tomorrow, you mean?" It's a running joke that Ace can't go a day without having at least one drink. "I'm actually shocked you're awake, considering it's barely ten in the morning," I can't help but add.

"Hey, I'm not *that* bad," he mutters. "Okay, maybe I am that bad. I have a meeting with my manager. I have a few big games to prepare for over the next few months."

Ace is a professional poker player, and a damn good one at

that. He can bluff like nobody I've ever seen. Back in high school, he used to clean up playing us guys. We all thought we were good, but Ace has always been in a league of his own.

"So, did you call to thank me for the party, or is there another reason?"

"I need a favor."

"I'm listening."

"The entertainment you arranged," I begin, "do you happen to have a contact number?"

"Do I want to know why you want it?"

"Probably not," I reply.

"I don't have a direct number," Ace admits. "Just call Valentino's and ask for Candy. She was the chick I arranged it through. Oh, and if you speak to her, tell her I want a refund. We were supposed to get two girls, not one."

"I'll be sure to bring that up," I lie.

Valentino's is a high-class gentlemen's club, located down the other end of the strip. I'm not usually in the habit of attending men's clubs—no matter how upscale they are—but I really want to find Ellie and make sure she's okay.

I call Victor, my driver, and arrange for him to pick me up downstairs. The club isn't far—just a few blocks away, but I really don't want to be seen strolling into a men's club. I'm hoping there's a back entrance or something I can use to avoid being seen, but no such luck. The only way in, as far as I can tell, is through the heavyweight guarding the front entrance.

"Here's fine, Victor," I sigh. He rolls to a stop out the front.

"Shall I wait, Mr. Stapleton?" he asks.

I nod. "Hopefully I won't be too long."

"Of course, sir," Victor nods, the faintest smile on his lips.

Lord, I can only imagine what he's thinking.

The bouncer straightens as he watches me get out of my car. When his eyes widen, I know he recognizes me. I narrow my eyes, confident that the second I walk in this place, he'll be on the phone to one of his paparazzi friends to get over here and snap a photo of me. It's a well-known fact that the Vegas Kings, as the tabloids call us, prefer our entertainment *delivered*. King and Asher in particular wouldn't be caught dead in a place like this, even before Lake was on the scene. Ace probably wouldn't care, and me? Well, I prefer to avoid paying for women altogether.

Reaching into my pocket, I retrieve my black Bottega Veneta wallet from my back pocket and pull out a handful of crisp hundreds.

"There will be another handful on my way out, providing nobody finds out I was in here." I give him a hard stare, so he knows not to cross me. "Are we clear?"

He nods. "Crystal clear. Don't worry, Mr. Stapleton, I've got your back."

I stroll inside and look around. I'm not sure if I was hoping to find Ellie in here or not, but I'm relieved I can't see her anywhere. I was pretty sure when we met that she wasn't an experienced entertainer, but she did seem pretty desperate for cash. Maybe that should be enough to send off warning signs in my head, but I just want to know she's okay.

A girl walks past me that I think I recognize as the other dancer from the party. Her outfit doesn't leave much to the imagination. In fact, she's wearing more make up than she is clothing.

"Excuse me," I say. "Are you Candy?"

"I can be whatever sugary treat you want me to be, baby," she purrs, a twinkle in her eye.

I smile at her and take a step back. "Sorry, I'm looking for someone specific. It's work related," I add, hoping she takes the hint.

She laughs. "You think I don't know who you are?" She tilts

her head to the side and studies me thoughtfully. "What would a guy like you want with a girl in here that's *work related?*"

That's a fair point, and if Ellie had any idea who I was last night, she'd probably be thinking the same thing.

I stop, when it hits me. That's why she stood me up. Someone must have told her who I am. She had my name. All she had to do was mention to one of her friends and she'd know my whole life history in five seconds flat. The tabloids and gossip columns just love me, which is partly my own fault; especially when I was younger and trying to rebel against my father. But I've been keeping myself out of trouble as of late—well, I had been, until a picture of me in Valentino's winds up in the gossip columns tomorrow. I guess that's all the more reason for me to stay until I figure out how to find Ellie.

"The girl who was with you last night," I say. "Is she here?"

"Oh, you're looking for no show?" she sneers. "Can you *really* picture her working in a place like this?" Her voice drips of sarcasm.

"Do you know where I can find her?" My jaw flexes, but I try not to show my frustration.

"Well, sure, but I'm not the kind of girl to give out sensitive information like that. I mean, I don't even know you..." Her lips twist into a smile as I reach into my pocket and pull out my wallet. "On the other hand, you *do* seem like a nice guy."

I roll my eyes and hand her a few hundreds. She nods in the direction of the bar.

"Ask Bea. She's her friend."

I wander over to Bea, who is waiting for me, her arms crossed over her chest, her heavily made-up eyes narrowed in suspicion.

"Jack Stapleton in a strip club," she marvels. "I thought you were too good for these places. Wow, you must *really* need an assistant."

I rub my jaw and let out a chuckle. "She told you, then?"

"She told me everything," Bea confirms.

"And you told her who I am, I take it?"

"Actually, no," Bea admits. "I was trying to convince her to go see what you were offering, but she wouldn't bite."

Wow. I'm shocked.

I slide onto one of the leather stools lining the bar and look around, noticing for the first time the huddle of dancers over near the stage, whispering and pointing at me. I groan and bow my head. I was a fool to think I could keep coming in here quiet.

"Can I get a drink?" I mumble to Bea.

"Sure. What do you want?"

"Give me a glass of Yamazaki, if you have it. If not, anything will suffice."

She turns around and grabs a bottle of Yamasaki from off the shelf. I raise my eyebrows, impressed. I was half expected her to serve me Canadian Club. I shudder at the thought.

"Anything else?"

"How about Ellie's phone number?"

"She'd legit kill me if I give you that," Bea winces. She casually places her phone on the counter in front of me and walks around the back, behind the bar. "Two, two, zero, six," she calls out.

I'm really starting to like this girl.

I pick up her phone, plugging in her password. It doesn't take me long to find Ellie's number. I put it straight into my phone and then I call my number on Bea's phone, because let's face it, it's pretty much a certainty that Ellie isn't going to want to talk to me. Unfortunately for her, I never give up, and I want to avoid having to come back for more advice from Bea. I nurse the rest of my drink and then get to my feet.

"Thanks, Bea," I call out.

"I don't know what you're talking about," she sings back.

utside, I wander down the strip in the direction of the hotel. The whole time, I'm questioning what I'm doing. Chasing women isn't me. I don't have to chase. Women love me. They fall at my feet in worship, begging me for attention. Sure, being an exorbitantly attractive, billionaire bachelor might have something to do with it, but I'm okay with that.

It isn't like I have time for a relationship, and the women I usually go for don't hang around too long. It's all about image and what my money can do for them. I'm under no illusion that any of the girls I've been with were in it for the long haul, but I get what I want out of it too. I get to combat loneliness without the complication of a relationship. I always have a warm body to keep my company at night if I want it.

Until now, that's been enough.

So why is Ellie any different?

I can tell myself I just want to be sure she's okay, but it's more than that.

I want to get to know her.

I bring up her number in my phone and press call.

"Hello?"

"You're late," I say when she answers.

She lets out a laugh. "Are you serious?"

At least she didn't ask me who I am.

"Very serious. We had an agreement."

"No, *you* had an agreement. I never said I'd come in," she retorts. "In fact, I think I made it pretty damn clear I wanted nothing to do with you."

"I don't take no for an answer."

"Careful with that. It might land you in prison one day," she taunts. "How did you even get my number, anyhow? Are you stalking me now?"

"Stalking is such a strong word." I grin to myself. "Honestly? I just wanted to make sure that you were okay. You seemed pretty distressed the last night. You were lucky I was there to help you out," I add, unable to resist firing her up.

"Oh, you mean your medieval attempt to rescue me?" she growls. "Well, thanks for checking up on me, my knight in shining amour, but I can assure you I'm fine."

The line goes dead, and I laugh, because that went as well as I thought it would. Partly my own fault, because I did poke the fire.

I dial Bea's number.

"I told you to take Ellie's number, not mine," she tsks when she answers.

"How did you know it was me?"

"I took a stab in the dark. Let me guess, Ellie wanted nothing to do with you?"

"She's feisty," I murmur.

"You have no idea," Bea chuckles. "She's also my friend, and I'll kill you if you hurt her. She's been through a lot, and it can be a challenge to get through her walls."

I'm starting to realize that, but it only makes me want to get to know her more.

"Say I wanted to, oh I don't know, *run* into Ellie somewhere," I muse. "Where and when would you suggest I do it?"

Bea laughs. "You're not going to give up, are you?"

"I never give up."

Bea sighs. "I have her working in the bar at the club a few nights a week. She has a shift here later tonight."

So much for never going back there.

"Thanks. I owe you one."

"No, you owe me *two*," she corrects. "And, Jack?"

"Yeah?"

"If chasing Ellie is just a game for you, I'll legit kill you."

"You said that already," I reply, but she's already hung up.

The line goes dead and I smile, sliding the phone into my pocket. I'm glad Ellie has a friend like Bea. It makes me feel reassured that she *is* okay.

I continue the walk to my office, my mood lifted. She can't ignore me if I show up at her work, but there's no way in hell I'm going back there alone.

I need some back up.

❦

"I'm sorry, I think I heard you wrong." Asher pauses dramatically before continuing. "You want me to go *where* with you?"

Valentino's," I repeat, enjoying his reaction even more than I thought I would.

He laughs. "You want me to go to a fucking strip club with you? Why not ask Ace or King? At least they'd actually get a kick out of going."

"Because I don't need the shit I know they'll give me," I groan.

"Okay, what's going on?" Asher asks. "You're acting really fucking weird."

I sit down and rub my hands over my face. The only way I'm going to get Asher to agree to go with me is by telling him the truth, but that's kind of difficult when I don't really understand it myself. Why can't I just let this thing with Ellie go? At first, I thought it was because I'm not used to women turning me down, but I don't think that's it.

I think I'm really into her.

"Remember my assistant from your bachelor party?" I say.

"Sure." His brow furrows. "Is she not working out?"

I laugh. "She was one of the entertainers that Ace hired. She freaked out when we were in the elevator, so I tried to help her out by telling you all she was my assistant."

"Okay, so what's the problem?"

"The problem is she was annoyed at me for ruining her gig, so I suggested she come work for me—"

"You offered a stripper a job as your assistant?" Asher stares at me in disbelief and then begins to laugh.

"She's not a stripper," I defend her. "I mean, she'd clearly never done anything like that before, the way she was freaking the fuck out."

"She was probably freaking out because she was on something," Asher frowns. "Seriously, man, I think you should leave it before you get even more invested than you already are." He narrows his eyes at me. "Wait a second, why do I feel like there's something you're not telling me?"

"I might've gone in there already to try to track her down," I admit.

"You went there?" Asher groans and rubs his face. "Dude. Well, was she there?"

"No. But I got her number from her friend who works there."

"Of course you did."

"And I called her, but she kind of shot me down."

"Because you're borderline stalking the poor girl," Asher groans, shaking his head at me. "And now you want to what, go back so you can accost her again? Trap her in a corner and make her talk to you?"

"You're making me sound like a real creep," I mutter.

"No, you're doing a stellar job of that yourself."

"Look, are you coming with me or not?" I'm getting annoyed with him now.

He groans. "You know Lake will kill me if I go anywhere near that place."

"So don't tell her," I coax him. "You owe me, remember?"

Asher sighs. "Fine. But after this, we're even."

⚜

*J*almost don't recognize Asher when he meets me a block away from the club. He's dressed in faded blue jeans and a sports jacket, with a pair of sunglasses and a hat covering as much of his face as possible. I chuckle to myself because the last time I saw the guy wearing anything other than a three thousand dollar suit was way back in high school. Even back then, he had a taste for luxury.

"I'm loving this new look," I tease him.

"Let's just get this over with before we're gracing the front page of the tabloids," he mutters, looking around us.

"Dressed like that, you're giving them more reason to chase us," I point out. "I didn't even know you *owned* a pair of jeans. I thought they were beneath you."

He shrugs. "They're Versace and actually super comfortable."

Of course they are.

I swear the bouncer smiles when he sees us walking up, probably because he knows he has a little payday coming his way.

"Mr. Stapleton. Good to see you again."

"Yeah, I'm sure it is," I snap, my tone impatient as I hand him some notes. "Same deal as last time?"

"You got it."

Asher glares at me as we walk inside. "You're paying off security now?"

"With you dressed like that, we're lucky I didn't have to pay double."

We step inside, and Asher groans. Every single patron is

dressed in a suit or similar. The irony is in his attempt to blend in, Asher stands out like a sore thumb.

"You could've told me it wasn't a bottom feeder kind of place," he mutters.

"You've never heard of this place?" I ask him, surprised.

He shakes his head. "Should I have?"

I shrug. I just assumed everyone knew about this place, even if we did avoid it.

I scan the crowd for Ellie, noticing her immediately. She stands behind the bar, facing away from us, her hair tied back into a ponytail. I watch, mesmerized as she reaches up onto the shelf for a bottle of scotch, the short skirt she's wearing rising up her thighs as her hips move along to the beat of the cliché music that blares from the speakers.

I nudge Asher. "There she is."

"Good luck. I'll be hiding in the men's room until you're ready to leave," he mutters.

Chuckling, I walk in the direction of Ellie. She's smiling as she serves a customer; probably because she hasn't noticed me yet. Three seconds later, when her eyes meet mine, my hunch is confirmed. A scowl replaces the smile, which is a pity, because she's so beautiful when she's happy. I'm starting to think her bad mood is me.

"You're here?" She blinks at me in shock. "How..." She turns around and gives Bea a death stare. "I'm gonna *kill* you."

"Just hear the poor guy out," Bea calls out over the music. She winks at me before turning her attention back to the drinks she's pouring.

"Your friend gives pretty good advice," I say, the corner of my lips lifting upward. "You should listen to her."

Ellie shakes her head. She isn't thrilled to see me, but she's not chasing me away either, so I take it as a win.

"What do you want, Jack?" She releases a sigh. Her eyes

look tired, like she hasn't slept properly in days. "If this is about the job, you can see I already have one—"

"Go out with me."

Her eyebrows shoot up, and then she laughs.

"You're asking me out now? That escalated quickly. What will it be tomorrow, marriage?" Her eyes narrow as she assesses me suspiciously. "Wait a minute, this isn't like those sappy romance novels, is it? Your grandfather isn't forcing you to get married; am I'm your easiest target?"

"No." I chuckle at the thought. "I can assure there is no requirement forcing me into marriage. All I'm asking for is a date."

She shakes her head. "I'm sorry, but I can't."

"Oh, come on." I slide onto one of the stools, hoping I'm making it clear I won't give up that easily. I rest my arms on the bar, clasping my hands together. "You're telling me you're not the least bit attracted to me?"

"I think you're *way* more in love with yourself than I could ever be," she murmurs, but the color spreading across her cheeks gives me some hope.

"Ah, so, what you're saying is that you *could* fall in love with me?" I tease.

"Stop putting words in my mouth." Her eyes roll upward, but there's a hint of amusement in them, which only spurs me on. "I'm not going out with you," she repeats.

"Fine." I put my palms flat against the bar and scan the liquor choices.

"Then I'll have a whiskey. Preferably something top shelf. And every single night you're working, I'm going to be right here until you agree to go out with me."

She snorts. "Good luck with that."

"One thing you should know about me"—I lean across the

bar, so my lips are almost against her ear—"is that luck is *always* on my side."

"Except when you're playing a twenty-one-year-old with a killer win streak, huh, Jack?"

I turn around to find Asher standing there, a smirk on his face.

Jesus Christ, am I ever going to hear the end of that?

"She was an amateur," I scoff. "And I let her win—"

"Sure, you did." He grins at me. "Now can we get out of here, please? Lake keeps calling me."

I nod and slide off the stool. I turn back to Ellie and give her a wink.

"Forget the drink. I'll see you tomorrow." I smirk at her. "And every night after that until you agree to a date."

CHAPTER SIX

The first night Jack came into the club, I was annoyed.

Even when he said he'd be back, I was sure he'd lose interest as soon as something else shiny came along, but it's been three nights in a row that he's sat at this bar, watching me as I ignore him. He's persistent. If nothing else, I'll give him that, and I can't help wondering...

Could he actually be genuinely interested in me?

It's Thursday night, and I'm at the club. Every two seconds, I glance at the door, waiting to see his face. When I do, something stirs inside me while my heart races. I wipe my sweaty palms on the side of my short black apron and take a deep breath. I don't *want* to be attracted to Jack, but I can't deny that I am.

"Seriously, this guy has no sense of self-respect," I mutter to Bea.

She looks up, spots Jack, and laughs.

"Cut the poor guy some slack. He likes you," she chastises me. "And for what it's worth, I think he has great taste."

"This is all your fault, you know," I growl at her. "Why did you have to give him my number?"

"Come on, Ellie. Look at yourself." Bea gives me a sideways glance. "You're a mess because you like the guy."

"No, I'm a mess because ... because..." I stop, glaring at Bea.

"Jesus, Ellie, just let your guard down and have a little fun with the guy." Bea throws her hands up, looking like she wants to smack some sense into me. "He's hot, he's obviously interested, and he's filthy rich. Do you know how many girls would kill for that kind of combination, myself included?"

"Then *you* go out with him," is my very mature comeback.

"I would, but he's not interested in me."

Straightening up, I force myself to focus on the pitcher of beer I'm pouring for a table full of young executives and not the fact that Jack's almost at the bar. I finally look up and meet his eyes when he slides onto the stool in front of me.

"Hey." He grins at me.

My heart pounds, because his lopsided smile is damn sexy...

Bea reaches over and takes the pitcher from me, then walks away, leaving me no choice but to acknowledge Jack. I hate that I've been waiting for him since I started my shift, and I'd love nothing more than to do what Bea said and let my guard down and have fun, but I can't bring myself to do it. I'm better off not getting involved with him. It's the only way I can ensure I won't get hurt. The problem is, it's hard to ignore him when my stomach does backflips every time I see him.

Like right now, for example.

"Back again?" I lift my eyebrows and meet his gaze. "People are going to start talking."

"Trust me, they already talk," he murmurs, his eyes burning into me. "And I told you, I'm going to keep coming back until you agree to go out with me. I always keep my word."

"I'm pretty sure it's against the law for you to do that."

"Keep my word?"

"Stalk me," I retort.

"There's a law against coming to the same club every night?" He pretends to be shocked. "The last time I checked, it's not a crime to look for a bit of entertainment." He flashes me a brilliant smile.

"The entertainment is over there," I say, nodding to Jilly, who's humping the pole on the stage. "Maybe you should turn your attention *that* way."

Bea snorts as she tosses her empty drinks tray in front of me, but Jack isn't fazed. His gaze stays fixated on me with an intensity that makes me shiver. I swallow and focus on pouring the drink in front of me as goose bumps prickle my arms.

"No, I'm pretty sure my attention is right where it should be." His gaze burns holes through me, and my breath catches in my throat.

Damn him and those sexy eyes.

"Is it going to kill you to agree to go out with me?"

I want to say yes, it *might* just kill me to go out with him, but I don't, because I know it's not true. There's a part of me that wants to give in, but I'm scared. I know the type of guy Jack is; he's the guy women swoon over. He oozes confidence, and he lives for the thrill of the chase. Once that's gone, where does that leave me?

I don't want to open myself up to the possibility of getting hurt. Not after all the pain I've endured over the last few weeks. Tears well as I think about everything that's happened. I turn around and clean the other counter, so he can't see the tears as they sting my eyes. I'm trying so hard to keep everything together, but him being here, hounding me is making it a thousand times harder.

I can't do this anymore.

I march around the bar and grab Jack's hand, ignoring the jolt of chemistry passing between us. He looks at me in surprise as I lead him through the bar and outside into the laneway that leads to a dead end.

"This is going somewhere I didn't expect," he grins.

"What's it going to take for you to stop coming here?" I demand.

"I told you already." All signs of humor disappear from his expression when he sees how serious I am. He stares at me, and for the first time, I see a vulnerability hiding in his eyes. "Go out with me."

"No," I whisper, even though I'm wavering.

"One date," he urges. He takes my hand again, the sensation of his fingers grazing against mine sending my body into overdrive. "*One*. And then if you never want to see me again, I'll leave you alone. I promise."

I hesitate; it sounds so easy. One date, and he'll leave me alone. The problem is, I'm not sure I'm strong enough to get through a date with Jack and not want to see him again.

"I always keep my word, remember?"

"Okay," I hear myself saying. "*One* date. On the condition that you go and don't come back here."

"I'll happily agree to that," he murmurs.

Neither of us move, and for a second, I think he's going to kiss me, but he reaches up and wipes away a stray tear that's managed to break through my barricade. I swallow as his fingers linger against my skin, every part of my body tensing. I think I *want* him to kiss me.

I step back, putting distance between us, before I do something I'll regret.

"I better get back in there," I say.

Without waiting for him to respond, I spin around on my heel and walk inside. He follows behind me, but I'm relieved when he heads straight for the exit, just as he promised.

My hands shake as I take my place behind the bar with Bea.

I glance over at the stage, where a group of the dancers and waitresses are huddled together. One of them scowls at me, then whispers something to the group, and they all laugh. I frown, because it's completely obvious they're talking about me.

"What the hell is their problem?" I mutter, my anxieties kicking in.

"Just ignore them," Bea says, glancing up at them before continuing pouring her drinks. "They're probably just jealous. I mean, you did take him out the back..."

"Not for that," I say, feeling mortified. Is that what they think, that I took him out back to do God knows what? I shudder and then turn my attention to another customer.

"So, what did he want then?" Bea asks after the customer has gone.

"A date, of course."

"I might be wrong, but I don't think the guy is going to give up," Bea warns.

I clear my throat. "I actually said yes."

She blinks at me in shock. "I'm sorry, but *what?* You said *yes?*"

I groan as she pulls me into a hug, which of course only draws more attention from the group near the stage.

"I only agreed so he'll leave me alone."

"Bullshit," Bea teases. "If you wanted him to leave you alone, you would've gotten a restraining order, like a normal person. You totally have to come to my place beforehand," she adds excitedly.

"Why?" I ask, confused.

"To get ready, silly." She takes my hands and hugs me again. "It'll be fun. We can drink a little wine to calm your nerves, and I can help you with your make up. This is so exciting!"

"Okay." I'm amused that Bea is more worked up about this date than I am, but her enthusiasm is contagious.

As my shift goes on, I find myself getting more excited about our date, especially since I have no idea when it's going to be. As if on cue, my phone pings in my pocket. Looking around to make sure nobody is watching, I pull it out to check the message, just in case it's Mom. It's not.

Jack: I should probably have asked... How's tomorrow night for you?

Me: Sounds good. I'll text you my address in the morning.

Jack: Great. I'm looking forward to this. Even if you aren't.

I bite my lip because I *am* looking forward to it.

More than I want to admit.

❦

*A*fter my shift, I head straight home.

I'm exhausted, and my feet hurt from running back and forth behind the bar all night, but at least it's a job where I don't feel like I'm selling myself out. Out of nowhere, tears fill my eyes. I know it's the lack of sleep having an effect on my emotions, but I'm so sick of everything being so hard. My life has been turned upside down and then ripped to shreds, and it feels like the blows keep on coming. Liking Jack is a complication I don't need right now.

It's nearly midnight when I pull into the driveway, and I'm surprised to see the house is still lit up. I turn off the car and frown because Mom should've been asleep ages ago.

She probably just left the lights on for me, because she knew I'd be late.

I can hear Mom sobbing softly before I even walk inside.

Shutting the door, I run through to the living room, where I find her curled up on the couch.

"Ellie." She smiles when she sees me and wipes her eyes. "I didn't hear you come in."

"Mom, what's wrong?"

I walk over to her and kneel next to the couch, wrapping my arms around her. She rests her head against my chest, her body shaking as she cries in my arms. I swallow my tears, because seeing Mom like this is breaking my heart.

"They were here again." She lifts her head, her swollen eyes meeting mine. "We have to pay up soon, or..."

She stops, but she doesn't need to finish. I know where it's heading.

"Were they in the house?" I ask, an edge to my voice.

Mom nods, still shaken. "I thought it was the food delivery guy when they knocked. As soon as I opened the door, he pushed his way in."

"He?" I rasp.

Mom nods. "The ringleader, the one who did all the talking at the funeral. He was alone this time, and he introduced himself. Snake." She lets out a bitter laugh. "What a fitting name."

My stomach turns. I feel sick because I should have been here to protect her, and I wasn't.

"Did they hurt you?" I ask.

Mom shakes her head. "No, but I don't doubt they will, if we don't do something, soon."

"We have to go to the police," I beg. "They can't walk into our house and threaten you. That has to be against the law—"

"Ellie, that's not an option," Mom cuts in. "Can you imagine what they'll do to us? They'd kill us."

"We can ask for protection or something," I argue, even

though I know in my heart that it wouldn't help. They'd still find us.

Mom shakes her head sadly. "We need to deal with this ourselves. *I* need to deal with it."

Her hands tremble as she lifts them to her face again to wipe away more tears. Her hair is a tangled mess, and she's long wiped off any makeup she might have worn with all her crying. But aside from shock and terror, she seems okay. I'm just relieved that he didn't hurt her physically.

"What are we going to do, Ellie?" My mom's voice cracks when she talks. "I don't know how much longer we have. My nerves can't take this anymore." She starts sobbing again. "Why did he do this to us?"

I shake my head and pull her close to me, soothing her like I'm the parent and she's the child. It doesn't matter what I say or do; it won't change anything. Dad got us into a load of shit and he isn't around to help us fix it.

Will they kill us?

Maybe.

"Come on, Mom. Let's get you to bed," I whisper, helping her to her feet.

She nods, and I help her to her bed and tuck her in.

"They won't come back tonight, will they?"

"We have a day or two before they'll be back," I assure her, and I actually believe it.

Beyond that, who knows.

After I make sure my mom is sound asleep, I collapse in my bed, but I can't switch my mind off long enough to fall asleep. If they were in our house once, nothing is going to stop them from doing it again. We have to do something to make this all go away.

The problem is, I have no idea what.

CHAPTER SEVEN

"Shall I get the next batch of applicants ready for you?"

I give Cindy one of my most charming smiles.

"Or you could make my life easier and reconsider your resignation?" She opens her mouth to respond, but I put my hand up. "I'm sorry. That wasn't fair of me. Yes, please get me more. None of these feel right."

She nods and goes to leave, stopping just before she exits my office.

"You'll find the right one, Jack," she promises, giving me a reassuring look. "You just have to be open to it."

"Open to what?" Piper, my sister asks as she strolls past Cindy and into my office.

She walks over to my desk and picks up one of the applications, peering at me from over the top of it.

"Ah, you haven't picked someone yet."

"It's a difficult decision."

"No, it's the easiest decision you'll ever need to make because any *one* of them will do," Piper laughs, waving her hands. "You could close your eyes and choose one, and it wouldn't matter because they're all very capable, or Cindy wouldn't have vetted them as an option. What's the deal, Jack?" Then her eyes widen. "Wait a minute. This is about losing Cindy, isn't it?"

"I have no idea what you mean."

"Yes!" Piper slams her hand down on the desk and flashes me a triumphant grin. "You're attached to her because she's the only mother figure you've ever really had. You think by accepting she's leaving you're losing Mom all over again."

I narrow my eyes at Piper. Only she could get away with talking to me like that.

"Oh, stop psychoanalyzing me," I growl. "That's not what's going on at all."

I'm annoyed at my sister. While there might be truth behind what she's saying, this isn't about me wanting a mother figure. Of course I'm not ready to let Cindy go. I've gotten used to having her around, and she knows how to do her job. All these young things, barely out of college, are only going to be interested in working out the quickest way for them to move up. I don't want to have to train someone else in a year. I just want...

I sigh. I don't know what the hell I want.

"You want me to make a decision? Fine." I snatch up the top application, scan it for a name, and then pick up the phone. "Cindy? Call Priscilla in for a trial please."

"Certainly," Cindy says, sounding shocked.

Piper screws up her nose. "Priscilla? She sounds like a cat."

"Don't you have work to do?" I snap, irritated.

She nods. "That's actually why I'm here. Vince needs a few weeks off because his wife had the baby early. I've promoted Cameron to head of gaming, but that leaves us short a Blackjack dealer, and we have that big poker competition coming up next weekend."

I nod, seeing where she's going with this. Any big tournament means an increase in clientele right across the floor, and

Vince is the main reason the floor runs so smoothly. Him being out throws everything off balance. I'm sure Cameron can do the job, but not half as affectively as Vince. Not only that, a week isn't long to train someone else to host the Blackjack table, especially when we need all extra staff to oversee the tournament.

"Okay, leave it with me," I sigh. "I'll figure something out tomorrow." I get to my feet and grab my jacket, aware that time is ticking away from me.

"Tomorrow?" Piper repeats, crossing her arms over her chest. "Why can't you take care of it now?"

"Because I'm busy," I shrug.

"When are you ever busy?" she presses, narrowing her green eyes. "You're a workaholic. You live for shit like this going wrong because it gives you an excuse to not address how pathetically lonely you are."

"Are you done?" I ask her dryly.

She shrugs. "For now."

"Good. And if you must know." I pause, long enough to wet my lips. "I have a date."

"A date?" she chortles. Her eyes light up when she realizes I'm not kidding. "You're serious? You have an actual date where you're not just taking a woman home for sex? With who?"

"Nobody you know."

I'm fairly confident Ellie doesn't run in the same circles as Piper, or anyone we know, which I'm happy about. For the moment, I want to keep things low key. It's taken so much work to get Ellie to even agree to a date, and the last thing I want is for those walls to shoot back up. I pause as a potential complication occurs to me. Usually, I'd have Victor drive us both, but I can see that being just the kind of thing to push Ellie back into her shell.

Maybe I can borrow Piper's car instead.

It isn't that I don't own my own car—I own several. The

problem is, none of them are worth less than a few hundred grand. If that didn't tip Ellie off that I'm someone of status, I don't know what would.

"Can I borrow your car?" I ask Piper.

"My car?" She laughs. "Why? And what am I supposed to do?"

I shrug. "You can have Victor."

Her eyes gleam. "Give me Victor for a week, and you have a deal."

"Deal." I nod, aware I don't have time to bargain.

❦

Back at my apartment, I feed Cat and then get ready for my date with Ellie.

Usually I'd don an expensive suit and tie, throw on my Rolex, and go all out to impress her, but instead, I choose a nice pair of casual Armani slacks and a dark blue shirt, then I slip on my Italian loafers and style my hair. I study my reflection in the mirror, satisfied, looking good but not too over the top.

Tonight, I'm not Jack Stapleton, owner of the hottest casino and hotel complex in Vegas. I'm just an ordinary guy going out on a date with the girl he likes.

❦

I park outside the address Ellie sent me walk inside her apartment complex. An out of order sign hangs on the elevator, so I take three flights of stairs to apartment thirty-four.

There's nothing wrong with where she lives—it's clean and safe, especially by Vegas standards, but it really hits home how different our worlds are. I grew up with a nanny, cleaners, gardeners, and everything I wanted was given to me. Not a lot has changed now that I've grown up. I've never worried about paying a bill, or whether I'd have enough money to cover my next meal. I'm ashamed to admit that for me, money is there to be spent.

Fuck, she's going to freak out when she sees where I live.

I stand outside her apartment, a rush of nerves filling me as I lift my hand to knock on the heavy wooden door. It swings open, and Bea stands there. My first thought is Ellie set me up, but then Bea stands aside and ushers me in.

"She'll be a few minutes. Don't mess this up," she adds, narrowing her eyes.

"How many times do I have to promise you I won't?"

Ellie walks into the room before Bea can reply. My eyes widen at the sight of her. Holy shit, she looks beautiful. Her long, dark hair is piled back into a messy bun, and the black dress she's wearing hugs her petite figure in all the right places. I'm at a loss for words, which doesn't happen very often.

"You look beautiful," I murmur, finding my voice as she walks over to me.

"Thanks." Her cheeks tinge pink. "You clean up pretty well too."

"Should we get going?" I reach out and take her hand. "Our table's waiting."

"Sure."

She's quiet as we walk outside, but I expected that, considering I had to all but force her to agree to go out with me. I'm not sure if she's nervous or just really not into the idea of me, but I'm hoping it's just nerves. I hope after tonight she realizes that I'm not such a bad guy.

I'm going to have to work for it, though.

"So, do you and Bea live together?" I ask, unlocking the car with the remote.

"No." She shakes her head and climbs into the front seat. "I just didn't want to wind up buried in my backyard if you turn out to be a serial killer."

"So... Bea's backyard is better?" I tease.

"She doesn't have one," she reminds me, a sparkle in her eyes. "And at least she'll be able to ID you in the police line-up."

I laugh, loving her sense of humor. I close her door and walk around to the driver's side and slide in. My hands grip the wheel as I turn on the engine. It growls to life beneath us, but it lacks the usual power I'm used to. When I drive myself, it's for a reason. There's no better thrill than slamming your foot down on the accelerator in a car that can go from 0 to 100 in sixty seconds flat.

We don't talk much on the drive toward the strip, but I'm okay with that. I'm too busy stressing over whether she's going to like what I've planned for her. I hope she appreciates it. It was hard coming up with something that would impress her without throwing my money around. Under any other circumstance, I'd go all out to impress her, but for now, I want to keep things simple and intimate.

"You're awfully quiet," I eventually comment.

She's barely said a word since we left. Then again, neither have I.

"Sorry." She winces apologetically. "It's not you... I just have a lot going on right now."

"Do you want to talk about it?"

"Not really."

I smirk; at least she's honest.

"Tell me something about yourself, then?" I suggest, trying to take her mind off whatever is bothering her. "Something unusual that I'd never guess just by looking at you."

She tilts her head thoughtfully, like she's giving my question some serious consideration. Then her face breaks into a grin, which makes my heart soar.

God, I love that smile.

"I have a thing for history."

"History?" That's the last thing I expected to spill from those gorgeous red lips, but to each to their own.

She nods. "I find it mind-boggling that humans have been around for literally millions of years, and we're all just going through the motions in our own little lives, oblivious of what it was like back then. When I was a kid, all I ever wanted to be was an Archaeologist," she confesses.

"Then why didn't you?" I ask.

"Money," she admits with a shrug. "I had the grades to get into whatever course I wanted, but it was a lot to money to put into an education that might not have paid off. Even with a scholarship."

"Not a gambling girl then, huh?" I tease.

I'm only joking, but immediately, she closes down. Any progress I'd made in breaking down her walls has been thrown out the window she's now fixated her attention on. I curse myself as an awkward silence fills the air. I'm not sure what I said that was so offensive.

"I'm sorry if I offended you," I say, feeling bad.

She doesn't reply right away, but then she turns to face me. Her eyes are filled with a mix of fear and sadness.

"My father had a gambling problem," she admits. "It ruined his ... *all* our lives."

Fuck.

Talk about killing the moment.

I just slaughtered this one with a fucking sledgehammer.

"I'm sorry," I murmur.

"It's fine; you didn't know." She gives me a forced smile, but those eyes tell me she isn't okay. I want to ask her more about her dad, but the last thing I want to do is push her away.

"You said he *had* a problem?" I say, praying it means he's overcome it.

"Yeah, well, he's dead now."

Well, shit.

"He killed himself."

Fuck.

This is going from bad to worse. How many other ways can I put my foot into it tonight?

"I'm sorry." I wince, because that's all I seem to be saying.

"The night we met at the hotel..." Ellie shakes her head. "His funeral was that same day."

"Wow. No wonder you were freaking out," I murmur. "And the dancing, was that because..." I stop myself, realizing what an invasive question I was about to ask.

That's none of my fucking business.

"Yes."

Wow. Ten minutes into our date, and I'm at a loss for words for the second time. I press my lips together and get ready to share something about myself. I don't usually open myself up on a first date, but I want her to know she's not alone.

"The day we met was the anniversary of my dad's death," I tell her. "He died two years ago."

"Really?" She glances at me with a frown, her eyes searching mine. "How did he die?"

"Plane accident," I say.

"Wow. I'm sorry."

I shrug. "We weren't that close, but it still hurt. It still does, but it gets easier."

"Everyone says that," she murmurs.

"The people you need to believe are the ones who have been through it too." I reach across and take her hand. She looks at me in surprise, but she doesn't pull away. "The worse thing was I didn't get to say goodbye," I reminisce. "In fact, I can't even remember the last time I told him I loved him."

"I told my dad the night before," Ellie murmurs, her voice so soft I can barely hear her. "The next morning, I found him in his car, in the garage."

I swallow back another apology, because I know it's not what she needs to hear. She stares out the window, shut off and distant again. A few minutes pass, and she turns to me again and smiles, like she's forcing herself to be positive.

"You never did tell me exactly what it is you do."

I groan inwardly. It's the question I've been dreading.

"You mean other than accost women and force them into dating me?"

Her laughter is music to my ears.

"Yeah, aside from that," she teases.

"I run a hotel."

I feel a stab of guilt for not being completely honest with her, but at the same time, it's so refreshing that she doesn't have any idea who I am. Ellie is the most genuine girl I've ever met, and I love that about her already.

"Wow, really?" She looks impressed. *If only she knew.* "That must be fun."

"It has its moments," I agree. I'm not even lying.

"Tell me about the craziest guest you've ever had?"

I don't even have to think about that one.

"One guy we had staying in the penthouse tried to sneak his cat in a few weeks ago," I explain. "The cat got loose and ended up running riot through the five-star restaurant, terrorizing the patrons and the chef."

Ellie bursts into laughter, the sound music to my ears.

"Oh my God, that must've been hilarious."

"Yeah."

I don't tell her the guy was me.

I pull into an old parking garage in the middle of the strip. Ellie frowns as she looks around. I chuckle at the uncertainty in her expression.

"I promise I'm not going to murder you," I can't help teasing her.

"I bet Ted Bundy said that too," she mutters under her breath. "Where are we?"

"You'll see," I say, getting out. "Trust me."

She gets out too, and I lock the car and guide her over to the elevator. The whole ride up to the top floor I can't keep my eyes off her. We step out, and Ellie looks around, taking in the abandoned, empty office building that at night is kind of fucking creepy. She looks at me with raised eyebrows.

"This is your idea of a romantic date?" She cocks her head to the side. "Wow, you must really want to impress me."

"Hold your judgment until the end, please," I chastise her.

Though I am starting to wish I'd just gone with my original idea of going all out. A helicopter ride over Vegas and then dinner in a top restaurant is looking pretty good right now.

"Sorry, I thought this *was* the end. You really built up an expectation and I have to say, this is kind of a letdown so far." Her eyes twinkle with a playfulness I haven't seen before. I take her hand and pull her into my arms.

"Oh, really?" I murmur. "We'll see about that."

I stare down at her, my eyes locked on hers. She's so close that I can feel her warm breath on my lips. My heart races. I so badly want to kiss her, but at the same time, I know what's awaiting us upstairs. Our first kiss will be much more special under the stars, surrounded by the Vegas lights.

"This way."

A flicker of disappointment moves through her expression as I lead her over to a door, but it's quickly replaced with curiosity when she realizes we're going on the roof. I go first, pushing open the door, so I can witness her reaction when she sees it. Her face lights up, just like I was hoping it would.

"Oh my God, that view," she breathes.

She gravitates over to the edge and gazes out, taking in the sparkling city lights. The building might be a shitty one, but the view is breathtaking. You can see everything from up here.

I clear my throat, and she spins around. Her eyes widen when she sees what's behind me; a table for two, complete with roses and candles. When the string quartet starts playing in the corner, her eyes widen even more.

"So, is this more like what you were expecting?" I ask.

"Definitely." Her eyes twinkle. "You set this all up for me? I don't even know what to say. Thank you."

"You're more than welcome."

I lead her over to the beautifully set table, complete with a pristine white tablecloth, the finest silverware and crystal glasses that sparkle against the fairy lights above us. The waiter steps forward, reaching for the bottle Don Perignon that's been chilling in an ice bucket beside our table.

I pull out Ellie's chair for her, and she sits. I sit opposite, watching her as she gazes around us in awe. The waiter hands Ellie her glass of champagne. She accepts it with a dazed smile, then he places mine on the table in front of me.

"This is..." shakes her head. "Wow. I can't even put this into words how perfect this is."

"I wanted to do something to show you I am serious about getting to know you."

"The fact that you wouldn't take no for an answer told me that already." She bites her lip to stop from laughing, then she looks over at the chef preparing our dinner in the corner and her eyes widen. "Wait a minute, is that—"

"Jaime Moore," I finish with a nod. "I'm lucky that one of the best young chefs in the county owes me a favor."

Jaime looks up and waves as he hands two entrées to the waiter, who walks over to us and sets them on the table. I wave Jaime over.

"Jaime," I say when he reaches us. "This is Ellie." I glance down at the plate of food in front of me. "And this looks amazing. Thanks again for helping me out."

"Anything for you, Jack." Jaime laughs. "I had one of the best wins of my life at your—"

"This guy a wizard with food," I say, cutting Jaime off before he can blow my cover. "Go ahead and taste."

I hold my breath as she delicately dips her fork into the seafood mousse and lifts it to her lips. Her eyes close as a sigh escapes her lips.

"This is amazing," she gushes.

Jaime laughs. "I'm glad you like it. I better get back and keep cooking. Lovely to meet you, Ellie." He shakes her hand and then heads back to his cooking station, leaving Ellie still marveling over the mouthwatering dish.

"My mom would love this," Ellie murmurs.

"Yeah?"

She nods. "She loves seafood. And this..." She shakes her head in disbelief. "This is next level."

"Jaime goes all out with everything he does," I agree. I'm not sure what I would've done if she were allergic to seafood. The way our date started; it was a real possibility. "So, are you close to your mom?

God, I hope she is.

"We're very close," Ellie says, her face relaxed. "We've always been close, but even more so now that it's just the two of us."

"I'm sorry about your dad," I say. "I didn't mean to be insensitive earlier."

"You weren't being insensitive." Ellie shakes her head. "You couldn't have known."

The conversation flows away from her dad, and I can tell that she's having a good time. She's opening up a little, although she's still guarded and distant. I can't blame her, though. She's been through a lot.

"How do you like working at the bar?" I ask, changing the subject.

"It's okay." She shrugs. "It's a job that means Mom can work less, but it's not where I want to be in twenty years."

"Where do you want to be?"

She laughs. "Realistically, or if money weren't an object?" she teases. "Realistically, I want a decent job, maybe in an office somewhere that pays well and offers good healthcare. If money weren't an issue, I'd go back to college and study archelogy."

I nod, impressed at how ambitious she is.

"You could always come work for me, you know."

I speak casually, hoping she doesn't take offense to my offer.

"I could, but that would mean we couldn't do this again..."

Damn.

She's got me there.

"Okay, so maybe I'm okay with you not working for me," I murmur.

Her eyebrows raise, a twinkle appearing in her eyes. "Oh, really?"

"If it means I get to kiss you," I add.

"Guess it depends on how much you impress me."

"I think you're pretty impressed," I tease.

"And you can tell that, how?"

"The way you react to my touch." I reach out and trail my

finger along her arm. She shivers, her eyes meeting mine. "The way you wet your lips when you look at me."

Shifting my seat closer to hers, I slide my hand around her neck, encouraged when she doesn't move away. I caress her face, then I gently press my lips against hers.

A gasp escapes her lips, falling into my mouth, but then she's kissing me back, her mouth melting into mine. She touches my cheek, her fingers electric against my skin. Eventually, I pull away, shocked at how good that felt.

The color in her cheeks tells me the feeling is mutual.

The conversation flows through the rest of dinner. Ellie seems to be enjoying herself more than I think she expected. I'm pretty proud of myself about that. She scoops up the last spoonful of her chocolate soufflé, licks her spoon, and then pushes her plate away.

"Good?" I ask as she sits back and releases a dreamy sigh.

"The best."

"Unfortunately, I can't take credit for dinner," I tease.

"Not just dinner; the whole night has been amazing."

She looks around, taking in the view again. I stand and take her hand, leading her over to the edge.

"See that building over there?" I point off into the distance. "That's my apartment."

"Right in the middle of the excitement." She shakes her head, her eyes lit bright with life. "I just love Vegas. Ever since I was a little girl, I've loved it here. The rush, the lights; there's no place like it."

I wrap my arm around her and nod my agreement. I couldn't imagine living anywhere else either, so it pleases me that she feels the same way. She glances at me and smiles, her gaze dropping ever so slightly as I reach out to touch her cheek.

I close the gap between us until my mouth is against hers. She kisses me back, showing me that she wants it as much as I do. Our tongues clash as she rubs her hands around my waist, tugging me closer.

"Thank you for a wonderful night."

"Thank you for agreeing to go out with me."

"Thanks for being so persistent." She giggles.

"Thanks for not taking out a restraining order against me."

She bursts out laughing, her cheeks tinged with color.

"I should get home." The mood turns sober as she pulls away from me, almost apologetically. I take her hand again, the chemistry between us electric.

"Or you could come back to my place?" I suggest.

She hesitates. "I should get home to Mom. It's so soon after Dad, and I worry..."

"I'll drive you home," I say, kissing her hand.

✿

I pull into her driveway in a nice, suburban street just out of the city. With its white picket fence and neat garden, I'm embarrassed to admit the house is nicer than I was expecting.

"I like your house. It's homely," I say.

"Thanks. But it might not be ours for much longer," she murmurs.

"Oh?"

"My dad ... the insurance wouldn't pay out because it was a suicide. Turns out he had a lot more debt than we realized."

"That sucks," I mutter. It's like this poor girl can't catch a break.

She smiles at me. "Yeah, it does. But you know what didn't suck as much as I thought it would? Your company."

"Ouch," I say with a chuckle. "I'm not sure if that's a compliment or not. You're a hard woman to impress, Ellie."

"Well, you managed it."

I get out and walk around to open the door for her. She gets out, accepting my hand, and then I lead her up to the front door. I feel nervous because I really want to kiss her again, but I'm not sure if she's ready for that.

"I really did have a great time," Ellie says. "Thank you, Jack."

My fingers still entwine hers as we stand there staring at each other, neither of us prepared to make the first move. I'm usually the king of first moves, but when it comes to Ellie I want her to want it as much as I do.

"I better get inside," she eventually whispers.

I lean forward. "Thank you for agreeing to go out with me." I go to kiss her on the cheek, but she turns, just in time for our lips to meet in a soft, gentle kiss.

"Can I call you?" I ask.

She smiles. "I'd like that."

✲

*D*riving back to my apartment, my mind is on Ellie. It seems she's the only thing I can think about these days. I feel bad for her, with all that she's been through. And now, she might lose her house. I click my hands-free and call Sergio, an old private investigator I used last year to find out more about my father.

"Mr. Stapleton. You're someone I didn't expect to hear from again."

"Sergio, how are you?"

"I'm good," he pauses. "I assume you're not calling for a social catch up?"

"No, I have a request. I need you to find out all you can on someone." I pause. "Or more specifically, her father."

"Okay, that doesn't sound ominous at all."

I laugh. "She's a friend whom I'm worried about. Her father committed suicide last week and left them with a lot of debt. That's about all I know."

"I can work with that can. Can I have her name."

I wince because I've just realized, I still don't know her last name.

"Ellie. I'm not sure of her last name, but I have an address that I'm pretty sure is registered under the father's name, if that helps?"

"Okay then. Text me the address, and I'll see what I can find out for you."

I pull over to text Sergio the details, and then I head home. My mind is still on what I thought was a pretty amazing date. The moment I walk into my apartment, Cat is all over me, meowing for attention.

"Hey, buddy," I murmur, scooping him up.

He purrs as I carry him into the kitchen and set him down near his food bowl. I scoop some biscuits out for him, then I get myself a glass of whiskey, watching him scarf his food down like he's never been fed. I'm pretty sure my housekeeper, Nancy, feeds him too, but I keep forgetting to ask her.

My phone buzzes. I pull it out from my pocket, hoping it's Ellie, but it's Sergio.

That was quick.

"Jack, it's Sergio. I've done a little digging, and I've found out some very interesting information."

"Wow, you work fast."

"It was pretty easy once I had the father's name," he admits. "It turns out Daddy has been *very* busy."

"Do I want to know all the details?" I ask.

Sergio laughs. "Probably not. If you're specifically after information relating to his debts, then you were right. He owed a lot."

"How bad are we talking?"

"Everything is behind. The mortgage is several thousand in arrears, but his biggest problem was the debt he owed a guy named Snake."

"Snake?" I repeat. "Who is he, a drug dealer?"

"He's a small-time loan shark. Usually chases things like gambling debts."

That makes sense.

"Oh, and just added curiosity. What's the last name?"

"Masters."

Ellie Masters. I smile.

I call King, knowing if anybody knows more about this Snake dude, it will be him.

"Do you know a guy named Snake?"

Silence.

"Yeah, the name does sound kind of familiar," King says a moment later. "I'm not a hundred percent, but I'm pretty sure he's a loan shark. If you're that hard up for cash, I can spot you," he quips.

"If someone owed him say a couple of hundred grand and they died—"

"Then the family would be pretty fucked, I'd say," King finishes off my sentence. "He has a reputation. Snake doesn't just threaten; he follows through."

"Thanks, man," I say and end the call before King can grill me for more information.

There's only one thing to do. The problem is, I'm pretty sure Ellie's not going to like it.

I shake my head; who cares if she hates me for it? Snake is a dangerous guy. If she stays in debt to him, God knows what she'll end up having to do in order to pay it back. I can fix all Ellie's problems in a matter of seconds, and my back pocket won't even feel it.

I call Sergio back.

"Sergio. It's Jack. I need you to do something else for me."

CHAPTER EIGHT

taring at the ceiling, I rub the grit from my eyes and release a yawn. My head is foggy from not enough sleep, mainly because I spent the whole night reliving my amazing date with Jack. When I first met him, I was sure he was just another rich asshole who was used to getting his own way, but last night convinced me that I was wrong about him. There's so much more to him than he lets on, so many layers that I can't wait to get to know.

The fear of getting hurt is still there, but there's something about him that makes me feel he's genuine. Like I can trust him.

"*Ellie!* God, Ellie. Get down here now."

The urgency in Mom's voice interrupts my thoughts. I jump out of bed and hurl myself toward the door, grabbing my bathrobe along the way. My first thought is they're back. Probably wielding baseball bats, ready to break some bones because we don't have their money. I storm into the kitchen, my heart pounding as expect to face Snake and his cronies, but it's just Mom. She sits at the table, tears streaming down her cheeks. I crouch next to her, not sure what's going on.

Maybe this has nothing to do with the money and she's

finally lost it. After days of trying to stay strong for me, she's finally cracked.

"It's over, Ellie."

"Don't say that," I hush her, anxiety bubbling through me. "We can still do this."

"No, I mean, it's really over," she weeps. "The debt is gone. It's been paid."

Huh?

"What do you mean it's all been paid?" I rock back on my heels and gape at her, confused. I'm sure I must have misheard her. How can it be paid?

"I mean it's been paid," Mom repeats, this time with a laugh. "Every last cent of it." She shrugs, looking as bewildered as I feel. "I don't know how or why, but we don't owe them a cent... I'm as stumped as you are."

I sit on the chair next to her and rest my elbows on the table, my hands clasped. Honestly, I'm not sure what to say. I should be relieved, but I'm not. I feel more nervous. Life doesn't work this way. Debt doesn't just disappear. Not for us, anyway. People like Mom and me aren't that lucky.

What the fuck is going on?

"We need to find out who did it," I finally manage to put my thoughts into words.

"Does it matter?" Mom asks. "It's done. Can't we just—"

"Of course it matters," I interrupt, shocked she doesn't want to know who would do this for us. "What if it's simply been passed onto someone else?" Mom gives me a worried look, like she hadn't thought of that. "Shit like that happens all the time," I continue. "They probably realized how hard it was going to be to get money out of us, so they sold the debt at a loss to someone else who wouldn't hesitate to cut off our toes or break our legs."

"Ellie, please," Mom cuts in, her tone harsh. "Stop talking like that."

I shut my mouth, even though I don't want to because I don't want to scare her, but as far as I'm concerned, the debt is still out there and not knowing who we owe it feels worse than before. At least we *knew* the other dude was an asshole. Who knows what our new owners are capable of? That's what it feels like. We've been brought.

"I know you're worried, but we have no reason to be. Snake promised me it had been taken care of. He wouldn't say by who, but he gave me his word that it was over."

"Because the word from someone named Snake obviously means so much," I scathe. "Look, I'm sorry, Mom. I'm just worried."

"Let this go, like I'm going to."

"This is *good* news, Ellie. Really good news. *Please.*"

"I'm glad everything is taken care of," I whisper as I reach over and squeeze Mom's hand. It's just hit me how much she needs this to cling to in order to move forward. But I'm not like that. I can't let this go until I know who paid out our debt. "I better get ready for work," I add, getting to my feet.

Mom smiles at me approvingly. "You're taking this job thing seriously."

I shrug. "Supporting us shouldn't be just up to you. I'm going to do my bit, so you don't have to work double shifts."

In all honesty, I would love nothing more than to give up working at the club and do something productive, like a course that would get me a decent job, but I can't do that yet.

Not until I know for sure we're okay.

Just because everything looks good on the outside doesn't mean it's not covering something more sinister. I learned a long time ago, when something looks too good to be true, it usually is.

"Actually, I better get going too," Mom says. "Will I see you later? We can celebrate."

"Sounds good," I say.

I kiss her on the cheek before walking back to my room.

✦

When I hear Mom leave, I sneak downstairs and into the study, where Dad spent most of his time. It feels weird being in here after everything that's happened. I swallow the lump in my throat and force myself not to think too hard about him, or I know I'll break down. 1os angry as I am at him for leaving us in such a bad situation, I miss him so much.

His chair still sits there, worn leather and cracks. If I close my eyes and think hard enough, I can almost picture him sitting in it. He used to hover over that desk, engrossed in his work, but the moment I walked in, he'd look up with a smile on his face, like nothing was more important than me. I breathe in the scent of his aftershave, his smell surrounding me. When my eyes are closed, it's like he's still here, like the last two weeks never happened.

But it did happen, and now I have to try to fix it.

Glancing around, I feel overwhelmed. To be honest, I'm not even sure what I'm looking for. Carefully, I rummage through the drawers, looking for anything that might point me to where I can find Snake. I know I should let this go like Mom wants, but I can't shake the feeling that this has put us in a worse position.

If I'm right and Jack figured out my dad owed some bad people money, I'm not going to stand back and accept it, but I don't want to confront him without some real proof either.

I pick up what looks like a drink coaster from a club. I don't recognize the name of it, but I look up the address. It's on the way to the bar where I work. Shoving it in my pocket, I quickly look around to make sure everything is where I left it, and then I walk out, closing the door behind me.

ell, this place screams seedy.

I stand outside the club, working up the courage to go inside. My skin is already crawling, but I suck it up, take a deep breath, and push open the heavy, metal door. It's dark inside, the stench of stale smoke and body odor almost enough to make my eyes water. Men covered in tattoos sit at the bar, looking me up and down like they're undressing me with their eyes, while their women, who I'm too scared to even look at, hang off them.

I quicken my pace before I lose the little nerve I have and make my way over to the bar. I'm almost there when I spot him; the man from the funeral.

He has to be Snake.

He looks over, his gaze locking on mine. His beady eyes darken as I walk toward him, my legs like jelly.

"I think you're in the wrong place, honey," he drawls.

"No, I'm pretty sure I'm right where I need to be." I keep my voice even because I'll be damned if I'm going to show him how terrified I am, even though my legs feel like jelly. "I want to know who paid off my father's debt."

Snake lets out a loud belly laugh. "What, do you want, a copy of the receipt too?" he mocks. "Shouldn't you just be happy it's done with? We both know there was no way in hell you or Ma were coming up with that kind of cash."

"How do we know the debt has really been paid and this isn't some kind of game?" I challenge.

Snake laughs an ugly, raspy laugh that crawls beneath my skin. "Do I seem like the kind of guy who plays games, little girl?"

"No." I shake my head and try another approach. "Look, I'm sorry. I'm not trying to offend you or make waves; I just don't want to owe anyone anything. Surely you can understand that?"

"I think you'd much rather be indebted to Mr. Vegas than me, honey."

"Who?"

"Jack Stapleton?" He throws his head back and laughs. "You're trying to tell me that a pretty girl like you doesn't know who one of the richest men in Vegas is? Owner of the Royal Hotel and Casino? None of this is ringing any bells in that pretty little head of yours?"

"Jack paid it?" I whisper.

"A rich guy like him would never deal with scum like me personally," he retorts. "He sent his henchman to deal with it for him. What's it matter, honey? It's gone. You can go on with your pretty little life."

I feel sick. There's no way in hell he's the same Jack.

My Jack.

And yet... It all makes sense. The hotel... God, he doesn't just manage a hotel. He fucking *owns* one. The Royal Hotel, where we were at the night of the bachelor party. I feel sick as it sinks in. Jack owns one of the biggest, fanciest hotel casinos in Vegas.

And now he probably thinks he owns me.

"Get out of here," Snake sighs, waving his heavily tattooed arm. "You're not my problem anymore, sweetheart. You're his."

"Thanks *so* much for your help," I say, my voice laced with sarcasm, then I turn around and head for the door.

"See you around, darlin," Snake chuckles after me. "Call me if you ever run into money troubles."

I storm outside, angry and not sure who I want to take it out on first; Jack for being such an asshole or Bea, because there's no way in hell she didn't know who he was right from the beginning. How could she not tell me the guy who was chasing me was Vegas fucking royalty? I'm so embarrassed that I didn't know. He must think I'm an idiot.

I decide to face Bea first, so I head over to her apartment. I run up the three flights of stairs and then bang on her door. She opens it, looking surprised to see me.

"Hey. Did we have plans?"

"Did you know who he was?" I demand.

"Who?"

"Don't play dumb," I warn her. I clench my hands into tight fists. I'm so angry I'm shaking. "Jack," I spit his name.

"Oh." Bea sighs, and then she nods. "Yeah. I knew."

"Then why the hell didn't you say anything?"

"Because you would have turned him down if you knew who he was, and I wanted you to give him a chance," she says.

"That wasn't your call to make," I growl.

"What's the problem? You guys went out and had a great time. You said so yourself."

"He paid off our debt, Bea. All of it."

Bea's mouth drops open. "And that's a bad thing?"

"Yes, it's a bad thing," I huff, annoyed that she doesn't get it. "It wasn't his debt to pay."

"It wasn't yours either," Bea quietly points out.

I close my eyes for a moment, trying to pull myself together. Sinking onto the couch, the fight suddenly leaves me. I'm deflated and lost now that I don't have my anger to hold me up.

"He probably expects me to pay him off with sex or something," I groan, covering my face. "I'll be sucking his cock for the next twenty years."

"Firstly, he really doesn't seem like the type and second, that doesn't sound like a bad—"

"Bea, shut up," I snap at her.

"Maybe he did it because he cares about you, and he was

worried?" Bea ignores me and continues. "Hell, if I had the cash, I'd have done the same thing."

I glare at her, but I can't be angry at her after saying something like that. Jack, however, is a different story. I hate him right now, and I hate the position he's put me in. I let out a growl, wishing I knew what to do.

"If you're that annoyed, go talk to him."

"I plan to," I say, my voice stiff.

Bea nods. "It's the only way you can clear it up once and for all. And then you'll stop taking your anger out on me."

I sigh. Bea is a good friend, who's always had my back. If she says she thought she was doing the right thing by not telling me who he was, then I believe her.

"I have to get to work," I say.

"Yeah, me too."

"I'll see you there," I say sullenly. "I might be a little late, though."

"I've got you covered," Bea says knowingly.

She's right about one thing.

I'm being a bitch to the wrong person, but I'm about to fix that.

CHAPTER NINE

The door to my office bursts open, and Ellie storms in. She stands in front of me with her hand on her hip, her cheeks flushed. I bite back a smile because I swear to God, I've never seen a more beautiful vision in my life—well, aside from the fact that she looks like she wants to slaughter me. She's pissed about something, and I don't need to think too hard to figure out what it is. She's angry I paid out her father's debt.

Cindy trails behind Ellie, out of breath. "I'm sorry, Jack. I couldn't stop her."

"It's fine, Cindy," I assure her. She nods and closes the door. I turn back to Ellie and raise my eyebrows. "You look upset."

"You think?" She glares at me, her blue eyes flashing. "How dare you go behind my back and pay off my father's debts."

"Ellie—"

"No, you're not going to talk your way out of this until I've said my piece."

She cuts me off, her voice so cold it chills me to the bone. I knew she'd be annoyed, but I figured I could sweet talk my way out of it like I do everything else.

"Who the hell do you think you are? Not only did you stick

your nose into my private life, *my* business, but you paid off my debts?"

"Ellie," I begin, but she isn't finished.

"Why are you so hell bent on trying to rescue me?"

She takes two steps toward my desk, her body tilted forward, her anger crackling around me like static. I stand because it feels weird to keep sitting when she's shitting all over me like this.

"Ellie, please, calm down." I know it's a mistake the moment I say it. If there's one thing you *never* do, it's ask an angry woman to relax.

"Calm down? You want me to calm down? All you've done is lie to me." She spits the words out. "And it's not only about the money, Jack. It's *you*. How long were you going to let me think you were just some small scale hotel manager?"

"For as long as it took for you to trust me?" I sit and motion for her to sit too. She glowers at me but sinks into the chair opposite me. "Look, maybe I didn't handle this as well as I could've, but I only did it because I was worried about you."

She purses her lips together into a thin line because she knows what I'm saying is probably true. I clench my hands into fists, fighting the urge to lean over the desk and kiss her. Instead, I continue trying to dig myself out of this hole.

"I know enough about Snake to know that you and your mom were probably both going to wind up dead at the bottom of a river by the end of next week."

That shuts her up.

She sits, the wind taken out of her sails, but the scowl on her lips remain firmly in place. Sighing, I run my hand through my hair, not sure how to fix this. I should've known she'd find out. She's not the type of girl to just accept something like that with no questions asked. I never thought she'd go right to the source to get answers.

Maybe I should've covered my tracks a little better, paid it off anonymously, but I wasn't thinking straight. I'm not exactly in the habit of paying off large debts for the women I'm falling in love with.

"How did you find out, anyway?" I ask.

"I went and asked him."

My nostrils flare. "You went to Snake? What the fuck were you thinking?"

"Of course I went to him," she snaps. "I had a feeling it was you, and I *hate* owing people. I was sure you wouldn't have told me the truth."

"You owed *him*," I point out, ignoring her dig.

"I was handling it."

"Exactly how were you handling it?" I question. "By putting yourself through something that isn't you? You hate the club; you said so yourself. And I'm pretty sure Snake isn't into accepting payment plans."

She sniffs, but she knows I'm right. Her fire is intoxicating. It is what I loved about her from the moment I met her, but I've never seen her this angry. It's a whole new level of sexy.

"Look," I continue, "If it makes you feel better, you can pay me back."

Her face sobers. "And what exactly am I supposed to do for you in order to repay two hundred thousand *dollars*?" she asks, her voice shrill.

"I'll find something for you to do." Her eyes widen, and I quickly shake my head. "No, god, nothing like that," I assure her, stifling a laugh. "I mean, I can give you a legitimate job. And if you don't want to be around me, that's fine. I'll give you something that will give us minimal contact. Okay?"

That seems to calm her down. She considers my offer, her eyes narrowing thoughtfully. I find myself willing her to say yes. Not only because I want her around, but because she deserves a break, and this is the only way she's going to accept what I've done.

"Fine," she says. "Find me a position that doesn't answer to you, and I'll work off my debt."

"Really?" I expected her to put up more of a fight.

"Yes," she huffs. "I don't have much of a choice."

"You always have a choice, Ellie," I murmur. Her cheeks flush under the intensity of my stare. "Be here tomorrow morning at nine. I have just the role for you."

One that takes care of my Blackjack dealer problem.

"I can't wait to find out what it is." Sarcasm drips off her tone as she turns around and stalks out, leaving the door wide open.

I lean back in my chair and sigh.

Well, I could've handled that better.

Snake was supposed to keep the details of me paying off the debt quiet, but I guess trusting his word was stupid on my part. The worst part is I know that any progress I'd managed to make with Ellie has been shattered. She has more walls surrounding her now than Fort Knox. Still, if I've messed up our chances of a relationship, I'll live with that.

I'd much rather that than leave her and her mom in Snake's hands.

My pulse quickens when my phone rings. I answer, hoping it's her, but it's Ace.

"Hey."

"You sound so happy to hear from me," he replies, his voice full of sarcasm.

"Sorry, I was hoping you were someone else," I admit.

"Let me guess. That assistant chick."

"Ellie," I correct. "And she's not my assistant. I decided to give her a more challenging role."

"There's something more challenging than putting up with your grumpy ass all day?"

"Watch it," I say, but I'm grinning. "Do you have a reason for calling, or do you just enjoy wasting my time?"

"Well, I do love to do that, but I have a reason this time. You're coming out with us tonight," he announces. "No arguments. We've decided you need to get your ass out of that office."

"Fine," I agree with a sigh. "I'll come."

"You can even invite that pretty little assistant if you like."

"I told you, she's not my assistant."

She also wants nothing do with me.

"Fine. I'll see you at Eight. Your sister's coming too."

"Piper?" I ask, surprised. She'd been hanging around with us guys a lot lately.

"You have another sister I don't know about?" Ace sounds genuinely interested.

"See you at eight," I laugh.

❦

Since we're headed to the same place, I offer a pick Piper up, and she accepts. Whereas I opted for an over the top penthouse, Piper lives in a mansion in one of Vegas' most exclusive suburbs, complete with sprawling gardens, tennis courts, and an Olympic sized swimming pool.

I can't believe she has this and opted for a BMW.

Victor pulls into her elaborate driveway and honks the horn. She walks out a few minutes later, wearing a dress I'm not too happy about my friends seeing her in.

"Don't you have anything a little more conservative?" I grumble.

She lets out a hoot. "Since when is it your business how

much skin I show? Besides, this is a two thousand-dollar Chanel dress. It oozes class."

"Fine." I concede. "So long as that's all that's oozing. What is it with you hanging around us lately?" I add, throwing her a look.

"Nothing." She shrugs and glances out the window. "I used to hang out with you guys a lot."

"I know, but then you grew too good for us, remember?"

She shrugs. "I guess I just realized how important family is, since you're the only person I have left now."

Even though I'm pretty sure she's manipulating me, I feel bad for questioning her. I know I'm not the easiest person to be around sometimes, because I close myself off. I never thought how that might be for Piper to deal with.

"And what about you?" she asks.

"What about me?"

"Come on, you've been going on secret dates, and from what I hear paying an awful lot of attention to a particular female, who you've yet to me introduce me to."

"How do you know all of this?" I ask with a laugh.

"It's my job as your sister to know everything."

"Well, trust me; there's nothing happening," I assure her.

"I get the feeling that's not by choice?" she teases.

"It's a long story, and I'd rather not go into it right now."

"Fine." She waves her hand dismissively. "We can save it for another night. Hey, let's do dinner. We can make it a regular thing?"

"Uh, sure?" I say, not sure what's gotten into her. "Come over tomorrow night if you like. I'll cook."

Piper laughs. "Since when do you cook?"

"Hey, I'm a new age guy." I pretend to be hurt. "I can manage to throw a few things together."

"I'll believe that when I see it."

❦

A few minutes later, Victor pulls up outside the front entrance of the Limelight Club. As always, there's a line of people waiting to get in that wraps around the corner, but we go up to the door and walk straight in. I don't think I've ever waited in a line in my life, and I don't plan on starting anytime soon.

We head toward the VIP room that is pretty much permanently reserved for King. He salutes us as we enter, but his eyes are firmly on my sister.

"Piper," King looks her up and down appreciatively. "You're looking hot." I narrow my eyes at King, but he just shrugs. "What? I can't help it that your sister is sexy."

"Yeah, well keep your hands off her," I mutter.

"I can look after myself; thanks, Jack," Piper retorts, flicking her long hair over her shoulder.

King chuckles and raises his eyebrows at me, but I stare him down. All the guys know my sister is off limits but King especially, because I know what he's like.

"Did you take care of your issue with Snake?" King asks, taking a slow swig of his whiskey.

I accept a whiskey off the waitress who's working our room and then sit on the plush velvet couch with a sigh.

"What were you doing with a guy like Snake?" Ace asks.

"It wasn't my trouble," I correct. "But yes, it's been taken care of."

King nods. "Good, you don't want to get mixed up with the likes of him.

"What did you do?" Ace asks.

I hesitate, unsure how much to tell them, but they're my friends.

"I paid off a debt Ellie's father left behind after he killed himself."

"You *what?*" Piper's eyes widen.

King pauses with his drink halfway to his mouth. Ace whistles through his teeth and Asher groans. I love how supportive my friends are.

"You know how to pick them, eh?" Ace chuckles. "This is the most a woman has cost you in such a short time. Well, unless you count Lake's friend Mauve—"

"Who I *let* win," I say through gritted teeth. "And it's not like that with Ellie. Trust me. She was pissed at me for paying off the debt. Stormed into my office and yelled at me kind of pissed. Can you believe that?"

"Are you serious?" King asks. "Pissed off about the cash?"

"She's independent."

"Or stupid," Ace says.

"Hold up, the fact that she didn't want some guy swooping into save her makes her stupid?" Piper directs her question at Ace, but it's King who answers her.

"No, I'm just saying if I owed a dude like Snake, I'd fall and worship at the feet of at anyone who paid off that debt," King explains to Piper. "Trust me, you'd never want to owe a cent to a guy like Snake." He turns to me. "Suicide, you said?"

I nod. "It's a mess. I feel for her. She's been through a lot."

Ace and King glance at each other.

"What?" I ask.

"Since when do you feel for a woman?" Ace asks.

"Come on, guys." I sprawl my hands out in a shrug. "Don't tell me you're heartless enough not to feel anything when you hear a story like that. It's a big deal, losing a parent and then sweeping up debt you didn't know about."

"Yeah, but you're usually black on white about this shit," King points out. "You don't *feel* for anyone."

I pull up my shoulders. They're right. They know me better than I know myself, sometimes. But with Ellie, everything is different.

"So, you're into this chick, huh?" Ace asks.

I pull up my shoulders and throw back my whiskey. I should have known this was coming.

"Yeah, so maybe I am."

Ace hoots and nudges King. "You owe me a grand."

"No chance," King responds.

"*Owe* him?" I ask, incredulous. "Are you fucking kidding me? You bet on me?"

"We sure did." He sounds proud of himself. "You thought we bought that bullshit story at the bachelor party? We knew she wasn't your assistant."

"Bastards," I mutter.

"Hey, the way you run without feelings involved when it comes to women is impressive," Ace explains. "We had to put money on it. King said you were going to chase her forever. I told him I give you a month before you give up and move on."

"Fuck you guys," I laugh, annoyed that my friends are having so much fun with my life.

"What?" King shrugs like he doesn't see the problem. "I bet on your side, dude. And I haven't lost yet. He's still chasing her." He looks at me. "You haven't given up yet, right?"

"No. Why would I?"

"Because you don't *do* love." Ace cuts in.

I open my mouth to argue, but King nods before I can.

"Yeah, this bet isn't going to fly if we start on love," he murmurs. "Hey, maybe we should change the terms?" He talks to Ace like I'm not even here.

"Hey, assholes," I protest, but they continue to ignore me.

"A grand says he can hook her before the end of the month," King says.

"I'm not *trying* to sleep with her," I try to defend.

"Done," Ace agrees, clapping his hand into King's extended one.

I shake my head and laugh. My friends are full of shit, but I'll let them have their fun, so long as they keep me out of it. Besides, chances of me getting anywhere with Ellie feel like they're growing slimmer. Every time I open my mouth, I keep fucking up.

She has to come around at some point, though, doesn't she?

CHAPTER TEN

*E*very time I think I have my life worked out, I get thrown a curveball.

At first, I thought *Jack* was the curveball, but now things have gotten so much more complicated. Lying to me was bad enough. Paying off my father's debt is something I'm not sure I can get past. In the end, we're still in debt; it's just to someone else. I frown as another rush of anger surges through me. He was someone I thought I could fall in love with, but how can that happen now when he'll always hold this power over me?

I put on a black pencil skirt with a slit at the back, a white blouse that looks formidable as hell, and a black blazer to match the skirt. I slide into a pair of low heels, slick my hair back into a ponytail and nod at my reflection in the mirror. I look exactly as I'd hoped; sensible, boring. I look nothing like I did working at the club, and I fucking love it.

Mom knocks on my door and pops her head in.

"Oh my, don't you look professional." She walks over, standing behind me to study my reflection in the mirror.

I smile. "Thanks. You don't think it's too... I don't know. Too much, since I'm not even sure what I'll be doing?"

I could be washing dishes in the kitchen of the hotel's restaurant for all I know. Then again, it's a three Michelin star restaurant. I'm probably *underdressed*.

Mom shakes her head. "I think it's perfect for your first real job. I'm so proud of you for getting out there, especially since it's been a tough few weeks."

I bite my lip, feeling guilty, because technically, this isn't my first job. Not only that, she has no idea that I'm paying back Dad's debt.

If she knew...

God, she'd kill me, and then she'd kill Jack.

Or thank him. I'm not sure.

I swallow, because I don't even want to think about what she'd do if she knew. I'm so torn, because on one hand, I hate Jack so much for continuously rescuing me. On the other hand, I'm so, so grateful that he'd do that for me. Confusing, right?

No wonder I'm such a mess.

Mom hugs me. "Good luck, honey. I know you'll do great."

"Thanks, Mom."

She leaves me to finish getting ready. I look in the mirror again and feel a pang of nerves. I still have no idea what I'm going to be doing. What if it's something really horrible, like... I frown, struggling to think of any position he could put me in that I wouldn't be happy with. My cheeks heat because even when I'm annoyed at him, the idea of being with him in a sexual way still makes me giddy.

When he kissed me the other night, I felt fireworks. Maybe it was where we were and being surrounded by the Vegas lights, but it felt incredible. I was finally letting my guard down and showing him a side of me not many people get to see, and then he went and messed it all up by trying to be my hero. Sighing, I grab my bag and stalk out. The sooner I get this over with, the closer I'll be to making our relationship level again.

Even if it is going to take me forty years.

✦

If I thought my nerves couldn't get any worse, I was wrong. Walking into the hotel lobby, my stomach is doing backflips. I look around, in awe of how lavish everything is. From the spotless white marble floors, to chandeliers hanging from the impossibly high ceiling, to the bellboys walking around in uniform, ready to pick up luggage before they're even asked. The first time I was here I was too nervous to take in how fancy this place really is. And to think Jack owns all of this? I cringe, feeling like a fool. How could I think one of the richest men in Vegas was just a lowly hotel *manager*?

Taking in a breath, I make my way through the lobby to the back elevators, which lead to the casino and the administration department. I exit on the first floor and walk through a walkway and find myself in the casino. I wander through, taking everything in. Not surprisingly, it's just as extravagant as the hotel. Extravagant and sophisticated. I shiver, a thrill rushing through me. It's also my first time stepping into a real casino.

I stop for a second and watch a Blackjack dealer at work. Men in suits line the table, all wearing the same unreadable expression as they watch the dealer intently. I watch her too, in awe at how skillful her hands are. She smiles at me, and gestures to the one free seat at the table.

"Would you like to buy in?"

"Uh, no. I'm actually here to see Jack Stapleton."

Saying his name fills me with butterflies. I try to swallow them away, but whether I like it or not, I'm excited about seeing him again.

"Of course." She points to an entrance at the side of us. "Go through there and keep going straight as far as you can go, then turn left. You'll come to a set of elevators, take one up to the top level, where you'll find his office."

I pretend that I'm mentally noting her directions, too embarrassed to admit that I've already been in his office. Yesterday, I was so worked up over what he'd done that I didn't take much notice of how I got there. All I did know was I'd managed to bypass the casino.

When I find the elevators she was talking about, things start to look a little more familiar. I press the button, and the door opens. It's empty when I step inside, but not for long.

"Hold the door," a voice yells out.

I push the button that stops the doors from closing, and a woman steps inside. She gives me a smile as she catches her breath.

"Thanks," she breathes, giving me a wide, friendly smile. "I practically ran all the way from my car. I must look a mess."

I nearly laugh, because from her perfectly styled hair and makeup, to her designer clothes, she looks immaculate. There's not even a bead of sweat on her perfectly shaped eyebrows.

"You look amazing," I blurt out.

"Thanks," she replies. "I'm late for a meeting I really can't be late for." She looks me up and down. "You look panicked," she decides.

"I do?" I'm surprised by that because I'm feeling good. Well, I was, until she said I looked panicked. If she thinks that, then Jack probably will too.

"Yep." She nods, studying me again. "You look like you're ready to hit that emergency stop button and run. Where are you headed?"

"To see Jack... Mr. Stapleton," I explain, not sure how I'm supposed to address him. "Today is my first day."

"Mr. Stapleton, huh? Wow, better you than me," she teases.

"Why do you say that?" I ask.

"He can be a total asshole," she whispers. "But you didn't hear it from me."

"Oh, I already know that. I've experienced it firsthand," I mutter before I can stop myself.

Her eyebrows lift, and she leans in closer to me. "Ooh, Now I'm curious. I was totally just messing with you. Everyone around here thinks Jack is great."

"Oh, it was nothing. My first impression of him wasn't that great," I babble, wishing I would just shut up, especially since I have no idea what this woman does here.

"I'm sure you'll love working here once you get to know everyone."

"So, you work here?" I ask, trying to find out more about who she is without being too obvious.

She nods, but the elevator door pings, and my new friend steps out before I can ask her any more questions.

"Well, good luck," she calls out, giving me a small wave. "And tell Jack Piper says hi."

After taking a moment to recover, I find Jack's office, only this time I wait to be announced, instead of storming in.

I suck in a breath while I wait, a hell of a lot more nervous than I was yesterday. Then again, anger makes a lot of things easier to cope with. The surge of adrenaline nixed my nerves, and I was able to storm into his office and demand that he speak to me. Now, everything is different. I'm not the one in control.

"Mr. Stapleton will see you now." The secretary smiles.

"Thanks," I say. I pause and turn back to her. "I'm sorry about yesterday."

"It's okay." She gives me a kind smile. "You'd be surprised how often people ignore me and just stroll right in there. Maybe I should've given this up years ago."

Jack's office door opens before I can reply. I take in a sharp breath as he stands in front of me, and god, he looks good. He's wearing a dark gray suit that I'm sure cost more than I'll be earning after a whole month of working here. Heck, his tie alone looks expensive enough to out earn me.

"Ellie." He smiles and motions for me to come in. "I half expected you to not turn up."

My heart races as I stand, my knees almost giving way. I force myself to keep it together as I walk past him, ignoring the jolt of electricity that rushes through me when my hand brushes past his. In his office, I take a seat and wait for him to do the same.

"I'm here, like I said I would be."

He nods. "You're probably wondering where I've slotted you in." His mouth lifts into a wide grin. "Get it? *Slotted?*"

"Hilarious," I deadpan.

He's not getting back in my good books that easily.

"Okay, I'll get right to it then. Ever played Blackjack?"

I shake my head. "No."

"I feel like you're intelligent enough to get the hang of it quickly. I'll have Cameron teach you the basics, and we'll see how you do."

"I'm not sure..." I stop and press my lips together. "After my dad, I'm not sure I could..."

Just the thought of gambling makes my stomach turn. Jack frowns. I'm not sure if he's annoyed at himself or me.

"I'm sorry, Ellie. I hadn't considered that—"

"It's fine," I quickly cut in.

I'm the one who wanted to work this debt off. If he wants to put me in charge of a Blackjack table, then that's what I'll do. I'm not even sure what caused my father's gambling debts anyway. For all I know, it could've been racing, or something completely unrelated to a casino.

"You don't need to do this, Ellie. I can find you something in the hotel—"

"I said it's fine."

My voice comes out shaper than I expected. I look at Jack, pleading for him to let it go.

He nods. "Okay then. You're not going to jump straight into dealing," Jack says gently. "To begin with, you'll manage the tables for me. Your job will be to make sure the dealers change at the right times, keep the floor safe, call security if needed. Things like that. Do you have any questions?" he asks.

I shake my head. It all seems pretty straight forward.

"Right," Jack says.

I shift in my seat, his professionalism making him even sexier than usual. He offers me a folder. I flip through the pages which stipulate my salary, hours, duties and everything else I could imagine.

"And the debt?" I ask.

"We can set up the details for that separately. However you want to work it," he says. "I have our COO on her way over now to take you to meet the gaming manager, who'll be looking after you."

I nod, the nerves beginning to set in. "Okay."

"It's good to have you here, Ellie."

The softness in his voice catches me off guard, because he's been so professional since I walked in here. I give a quick nod and stand when the door opens.

"Ellie, this is Piper, our Chief of Operations," Jack says. "She pretty much runs the casino for me."

"I wouldn't say that ... wait, who am I kidding? Of course I would."

I turn around, recognizing the voice instantly.

Oh, please no.

But there she is, the woman I met in the elevator.

"Hi." I plaster a smile on my face, but inside, I'm dying.

"Piper is also my sister," Jack confesses.

My stomach drops. This just keeps getting worse.

"Ah, Ellie and I have already met." She grins broadly and motions for me to follow her.

As soon as we're out of the office, I let out a breath I didn't know I was holding. Piper looks at me and laughs, which only makes me feel worse. All I can think about is what I said about Jack.

God, what if she tells him?

Does it matter? He already knows I think he's an asshole.

"I'm sorry about earlier. I didn't know you were his sister," I say, cringing.

"Obviously," Piper laughs. "And it's okay. Jack *can* be an asshole. But in all seriousness, my brother is a good guy. Really," she adds. "Let's start again." She extends her perfectly manicured hand. "Hi, I'm Piper."

"Hi, Piper; I'm Ellie." I play along, even though I feel foolish standing in an elevator, reintroducing myself to someone I've already met, especially when we're standing in the same spot of our original encounter.

"So, you and my brother." Piper's brown eyes narrow. "I sense a story brewing there."

"It's nothing," I quickly reply. "I've just heard a lot about him in the media."

I'm babbling, like I do when I'm nervous and hoping she buys my story enough to stop asking questions. The last thing I want is for everyone to know the real reason I'm working here. Not that I think Piper would tell anyone, even if she did find out.

"Uh huh." From her raised eyebrows, I can tell she doesn't believe me. Lucky for me, the doors spring open before she can ask me any more questions.

"Before I take you to Cameron, I'll show you around."

Ten minutes later, I've learned everything I need to know,

from where I clock on and off my shift, where I have my break, to who I go to if I have a complaint. The last one makes me smile, because I couldn't imagine taking any issues I have to anyone other than Jack.

But I work for him now, so I can't go doing things like that.

The best thing I can do for both of us is just avoid him as much as possible.

⚜

By the end of my first shift, I'm both exhausted and excited. I'd never admit it to Jack, but I'm so grateful to have been given this opportunity. I love learning new things, and Blackjack is a very technical game with a lot of rules that requires plenty of skill and a whole lot of luck. There's so much to learn and remember, but I feel like I'm doing okay.

I gather my things from the staff room and head across the casino floor to the exit. My brain feels like mush after concentrating so hard to take everything in, but it's been such a fun day.

As I walk outside, I glance up at the large windows in front of Jack's office. I'm surprised to see him looking down at me, His hands tucked into his pockets, he smiles at me in a way that makes my heart race. I smile back, then climb into my car.

My phone buzzes as I go to start my car. I fish it out of my pocket and smile when I see a text from Jack. I don't want to be excited to hear from him, but I can't help the way he makes me feel. As much as I want to be angry at him, I'm wavering. He did a wonderful thing for us because he thought we were in danger. I should be grateful instead of fighting him on it, because at the end of the day, he's right. Guys like Snake don't mess around.

Jack: So... Am I still in the bad books?

standing there, eyeing me suspiciously. I shove my hands in my pockets and try to look casual, but she isn't buying it. She walks over to the window, spots Ellie getting into her car, and laughs.

"Do you do this every day?"

"No," I snap, but then I shrug. "Just most days."

"Why don't you go talk to her like a normal person?"

"Because she doesn't want anything to do with me."

I sigh and sink back in my chair.

"She's taking the no fraternizing at work policy so far that she won't even be in the same room as me. Not that we've had many opportunities to be in the same room."

"You're the boss. Make it happen."

"And that doesn't sound creepy at all," I retort. "How's everything going over there anyway?" I ask. Piper is my eyes and ears when it comes to the casino and its every day running.

"Smooth, as always," she says with a smirk. "Are you asking about anything in specific?" Her eyes twinkle. "Like a certain new Blackjack hostess, for example?"

I pull up my shoulders into a shrug. "What? It's not like I'm trying to hide that I like her."

"You'd be doing a lousy job if you were," she cracks.

"I just want to know if she's fitting in."

I don't want to go into detail about her father and give Ellie another reason to hate me, but I still feel bad about throwing her into the deep end without any consideration to how it might make her feel.

"She's getting there," Piper says.

She kicks off her shoes and sits, placing her feet on the edge of my desk. She treats my office like her own private retreat, even though she has her own, which is just as fancy. Not that I'm complaining. I like our little catch ups, especially when they let me check up on Ellie without looking like a creep.

"Her biggest problem is she lacks confidence. No idea why, because she's damn good at it."

"Really?" I'm pleased to hear that.

Piper nods. "She's running her own table now. She's taken to it like nothing I've seen before. She's smart and innovative. She's a really good addition to the team. I'm pretty sure she's enjoying it, too."

I'm grinning from ear to ear, and I don't even care. I love hearing that she's enjoying herself.

"So, are you going to tell me what's going on between the two of you?" Piper asks.

"Nothing's going on between us," I hedge.

"Come on, Jack," she coaxes. "You know you can tell me anything. Ellie wouldn't have called you an asshole for no reason."

"She called me that?" I'm not sure I trust my sister, who shrugs innocently. "If she did, I'm not sure why. Nothing's going on."

"Sure there isn't," Piper teases. "That's why you were pressed against the window when I walked in here. Why don't you ask her out on a date?" Piper asks.

"I told you, she won't have anything to do with me because I'm her boss. And I took her on a date already," I admit, not sure why I'm opening up now, after insisting there was nothing going on between us.

"Ah, the plot thickens," Piper giggles and gives me a devious look. "Don't tell me you've lost your charm, big brother."

"I haven't lost my charm," I retort. "She's just ... different."

"Different to the bimbos you normally have chasing you." Piper sniggers.

"Shouldn't you be getting back to work?"

"You're right. I wouldn't want the boss to fire me." She

pushes her feet into her heels with a wince. As stands, she smiles at me. "For what it's worth, I'm glad Ellie's a challenge," she says, her voice sincere. "Life gets boring when everything falls into your lap."

Piper leaves me alone to ponder what she said. She's right, challenge is good, but Ellie is more than that. For once in my life, this isn't about the thrill of the chase. I want to get to know her and spend time with her.

If I want to be with her so bad, then why the fuck aren't I trying harder?

Picking up my phone, I dial her number, my heart beating a little faster when she answers. God, I've missed the sound of her voice.

"Yes?"

"You sound suspicious," I acknowledge.

"Because my boss is calling me. Every TV show I've watched has taught me when the boss calls, it's a bad sign."

"I wanted to check how you're settling in."

"Like you did yesterday?" she teases. "And you think I don't know you have your sister checking up on me?"

"Busted," I chuckle. "But seriously, how are you going?"

"It's great. Really. I'm enjoying myself."

"And the—"

"I'm handling that," she cuts me off, her voice soft. "I think it's helping in a weird way. Forcing me to face some issues and stuff." She hesitates. "Look, Jack, I appreciate the call, but I think I should go. I also think... Maybe it's not the best idea for you and I to keep texting each other."

"If that's what you want."

I am her boss. The last thing I want is for her to feel uncomfortable, but the idea of having no contact with her at all makes me feel like shit.

"It's not what I want. It's what's best." She pauses. "I like talking to you, but it isn't very professional. What if people found out and thought I was using you to advance my career?"

"Who cares what people think?"

"I do." She sighs. "You're the boss. It's easy for you. I'm just another one of your many employees, and I think that's how we should keep it."

"Okay. I'll let you get back to work then."

"You're angry," she observes.

"No, I'm just … disappointed." I sigh, trying to put my feelings into words. "I get it, Ellie. I do. It's fine. From now on, we'll keep things professional. Have a nice night."

I end the call before she can comment and get back to work, doing my best to pretend I'm not fazed by her request.

By seven, I've finished the tasks I had set for the day, and I'm ready to go home and relax. When I step into the elevator, Ellie is there.

"Fancy running into you here."

She looks up in surprise, the awkwardness between us obvious after our phone call earlier. I press the ground floor and wait for the doors to close. Ellie edges closer to the far wall, putting as much distance between us as possible.

"You're working late," I comment, knowing her shift finished an hour ago.

"Cameron was running through some things for me. There's a big competition this weekend that he wants me prepared for."

I nod. I'd forgotten about that.

"How are you managing so far?" I ask, even though I asked her the same question on the phone earlier.

"You asked me that before. Remember?" Her voice is teasing.

I stifle a groan, because I fucking hate that our relationship has been reduced to small talk. Next thing we'll be taking about the weather. Even our first date wasn't weird like this, so why the fuck is it so awkward now?

Because you like her.

"I take back what I said about being okay with keeping things professional," I growl. "Go out with me again."

Ellie's eyes widen with surprise. Her lips part, and I brace myself for another rejection, but before she can, the elevator comes to a jerking halt. Panicked, Ellie grabs onto my side to keep her balance as the elevator shutters around us, then everything goes black.

"Fuck," she whispers through the darkness.

"It's okay. I'm going to sit you on the floor," I say, guiding her down. "I have an emergency deadlock on these elevators. We might be stuck in here for a while, but I promise we'll be okay."

Using the flashlight on my cell, I hit the emergency button and wait for the phone call. Within thirty seconds, the phone rings.

"This is maintenance," Charlie's gruff voice spills down the line.

"Hey, Charlie. It's Jack Stapleton. I'm stuck in elevator two. It stopped suddenly between levels four and five. I'd appreciate you getting us out as quickly as possible."

"Of course, sir. We'll get on it right away."

"See?" I say to Ellie, hanging up the phone. "Everything is fine."

Ellie nods, but she still looks nervous. I sit next to her, keeping the flashlight on and take her hand.

"Let's take your mind off things. How about a game?"

"A game?" She looks at me in disbelief."

"Sure—"

I stop when there's another shudder. Her grip on my hand tightens to the point where I'm losing circulation. Not that I care much. I'm just enjoying being this close to her.

"Relax," I soothe her. "We'll be fine, I promise."

She shifts closer to me so she's almost sitting in my lap. I put my arm around her, which she seems to like.

"How is your mom holding up?" I ask, trying to take her mind off things.

"She's doing okay," Ellie mumbles. "Thanks to you."

I shake my head, even though she can't see me. "All I did was take out the unnecessary pressure. Dealing with loss isn't easy. You're both so strong."

Ellie sighs. "Can I be honest with you?"

I nod. "You can tell me anything."

She nods. "I don't always feel like I'm so strong and so on top of it. I act like I am for my mom's sake. But sometimes it's just heavy. You know?"

I know what it's like to have to be strong, when on the inside I feel like I'll disappear like fog in the morning light, but I don't know how to take her pain away.

"I know it's always easy to say, but it does get better."

"Yeah, everyone says that. I just don't see how it can hurt less as time goes on. I mean, the facts don't change. My dad is still dead, and he still lied to us."

I think about that for a moment. "I guess it doesn't get easier, and the pain doesn't go away either. You just learn how to carry it better. You become stronger."

Silence.

"That makes sense." She sounds calmer. "I appreciate you listening to me, Jack."

"Anytime."

I mean it in the truest sense of the word. She could come to me with anything, and I'd listen. For the next little while, the conversation flows, the way it did on our date. The awkwardness that's been floating between us over the last few weeks feels long gone.

"You're different than I thought you'd be," Ellie says.

"Different how?"

"You're not an asshole."

I laugh. "Ah, so Piper wasn't kidding."

"She told you?" Ellie groans.

"She also said you told her I was a pretty good kisser."

"She did *not*," Ellie gasps.

"No," I murmur. "But I have you thinking about it now, don't I?"

I can't help myself. I lean in and press my lips to hers. She freezes for a moment, but then she melts against me and sighs into my mouth. Surrounded by complete darkness, my other senses are heightened. I cup her chin and slide my tongue into her mouth, tasting her, exploring her. We kiss for what feels like hours. It's like we can't get enough of each other. The lights come back on mid-kiss. She pulls away, her cheeks flush with embarrassment. I stand and put my hand out, helping her to her feet.

"Jack—"

She stops when the doors suddenly open onto the ground floor. She glances back at me then grabs her back, giving me an apologetic look.

"I have to go."

I sigh, feeling like I've fucked everything up again. The elevator phone rings. I pick it up, knowing it will be Charlie, checking everything is alright.

"Thanks, Charlie," I mutter.

"You're welcome, boss." He pauses for a moment. "You do realize we have cameras in the elevators, right? Those fancy ones with night sensors?"

Fuck. Of course we do.

"Thanks for the heads-up," I chuckle.

I hang up the phone and walk out to the parking lot. Piper

still has Victor, so today I have my Maserati. My phone vibrates as I climb in. I pull it out and smile because it's from Ellie.

Ellie: You're a great kisser, but that doesn't mean I'll go out with you again.

Tossing the phone on the passenger seat, I can't help but smile.

I'll change her mind if it's the last thing I do.

CHAPTER TWELVE

I pull into a bay in the staff parking lot, then cut the engine. I don't get out right away. I take a moment to reflect on everything that's happened in such a short space of time. My dad, Jack, and how I've ended up here, doing something that I'm actually pretty good at. I never considered working in a casino might be something I'd enjoy, even before Dad, but this place has changed that for me. I'm paying Jack back, and I know the money I'm making is helping Mom a lot. We've actually managed to catch up on the mortgage payments, which means we might not lose the house. Things finally feel like they're coming together. Or at least they were, until Jack kissed me last night.

The moment I walk out on the floor, Cameron approaches me. He looks even more stressed than usual. I glance at my watch to make sure I'm not late. I'm ten minutes early.

"Ellie, thank god." He gasps in his usual dramatic tone. "Jack wants to see you."

I blink at him. "He does?"

My stomach shifts because whatever the reason he wants to see me, being alone with him in his office is not a good idea.

Cameron mistakes my unease for worry and gives me an encouraging pat on the back.

"Relax, kid. He probably just wants to see how you're settling in. I already told him you're the best decision he's ever made." Cameron offers me a warm smile. "When you're done up there, come find me. We'll go over the program for the competition again."

I nod. "Thanks, Cameron."

I leave the floor and head straight for Jack's office. When I reach the elevator, I nervously step inside. I know it wouldn't be operating if it wasn't fixed, but after yesterday, I can't help but worry.

When I step onto the plush carpet that stretches all the way from the elevator to the secretary's desk, Cindy looks up at me and smiles.

"You can go straight in." She nods at the door. "He's waiting for you."

He's waiting for me...

My heart aches at the thought.

Taking a deep breath, I knock on the door. He acknowledges me with a nod, and I twist the knob and walk inside, closing the door behind me.

"You wanted to see me?"

My stomach flutters with nerves, no matter how much I wish it didn't. It's one thing to convince myself that liking him is a bad idea when I'm alone, but when I'm front of him, I lose sense of everything. Jack stands and walks around his desk, sitting on the edge of it. He motions for me to take a seat. I do, aware of how close he is to me.

"I missed you," he murmurs.

I blink at the confession, his words so simple and honest.

"I assume I'm not here for a performance review, then?" I ask.

Thank God I'm sitting, or I'd be at risk of my knees giving way. His cologne is intoxicating, he's so close to me. He leans a little closer, and my breath catches.

"Depends..." he whispers. "Are you referring to your performance on the Blackjack floor or in my elevator?"

My cheeks heat, and I'm sure I'm blushing furiously. Jack chuckles, his smooth voice sending shivers down my spine. God, I want him to kiss me again so bad.

"So, you missed me. What makes you think I missed you?"

"The way you're blushing right now kind of gives you away."

"Don't flatter yourself. I blush over anything. And for the record, you kissed me in the elevator. A *real* gentleman man would take that hint and leave well enough alone when a woman makes it clear she isn't interested."

"There's nothing gentlemanly about me." Jack's eyes twinkle. "And I'm pretty sure you kissed me back. With tongue," he adds, for good measure.

Jack leans forward, closing the small gap between us, and presses his lips against mine, sending sparks through my body. I kiss him back, letting my tongue explore his mouth. My heart races. This guy has me feeling things I've never felt before, and it scares the heck out of me.

"See, I'm not really getting the *leave me alone* vibe," he murmurs when he breaks the kiss.

"Yeah," I breathe. "I guess I need to work on that."

He chuckles at the back of his throat, his eyes growing a darker, more intense shade of blue, then he slides his arm around my waist and pulls me tightly against him. When he kisses me again, I moan softly, his tongue slipping into my mouth. He pulls back but doesn't let go of me.

"Come over to my place for dinner tonight," he whispers. "Just dinner," he promises. "I'll cook."

"You cook? I'm surprised you don't have a personal chef," I tease.

"I do have one, but I'll give him the night off. I actually enjoy cooking. I just don't have enough time for it." He pulls me forward and plants another kiss square on my mouth. "So is that a yes?"

"Yes," I say in a voice that's as unstable as I feel.

He grins at me. "I'll text you my address."

"Am I free to go back to work now? Cameron will be wondering where I am."

"Cameron loves you." He smirks. "It's a good thing Cameron is happily married, or I'd be a very jealous man."

I giggle, liking the idea of him being jealous of another man paying attention to me.

"Go," he urges. "Before I do something we'll both regret."

I'm not game enough to ask him what that is or admit that part of me wants to find out. Walking out of his office, I give Cindy a wave as I walk past her desk and head back to the elevator. I take a deep breath, trying to steady my emotions.

It's hard, though, when they're all over the place.

The rest of the day goes by in a daze, and before I know it, I'm on my way home. Mom is at the kitchen table when I walk in. I kiss her on the cheek, and she narrows her eyes.

"You seem more chipper than usual." She peers at me over the rim of her teacup.

I roll my eyes. "Am I ever really chipper?"

"Now that I think about it, you're much happier since you started your new job," she continues, ignoring my comment.

I pour a glass of orange juice and drink it, whilst leaning against the counter.

"What can I say?" I shrug. "I'm really enjoying it. I would never have thought overseeing a game of Blackjack could be so fulfilling."

"So is there someone specific that's putting that giddy smile on your face?"

"No," I reply, but my cheeks are hot.

"Could my daughter have a crush on someone?" Mom teases. "Who is he, a colleague?"

"There is no crush," I insist, my cheeks heating. "Can't I just be happy things finally feel like they're going right for us?"

"Of course, you can. And if you don't want to tell me about the boy, you don't have to."

I snort because Jack is far from a boy, but I let it go. I'm not ready to tell her about him just yet. Not until I'm sure what we have is real.

I excuse myself and head to my room to get ready. I'm about to step into the shower, when I get a text from Bea. I feel bad because it's been ages since we caught up.

Bea: Yo. Are you okay?

Me: Yes, I'm sorry. I've been so busy with work. Catch up tomorrow? Lunch?

Bea: Sounds great x

*A*fter my shower, I dress in a deep red dress that I bought for a Valentine's party I never went to. It's strapless, short, and very cute, stopping just above my knee. I slide on some ballerina flats, put on some makeup and tie my hair back into a messy bun. I glance at my reflection in the mirror and smile.

Perfect.

Mom looks up when I walk back into the kitchen.

"You look nice. Going out?"

"I'm having dinner with Bea," I fib.

I feel bad lying to her, but I convince myself it's for my own good. I guess on some level I still expect this thing with Jack to implode. The last thing I need is Mom pitying me. It's a horrible way to look at our relationship before it's even really started, but I can't help it. I've been hurt too many times.

"Have a good night, sweetheart," my mom says when I walk toward the door.

"You too," I say with a smile.

I'm sure I will.

CHAPTER THIRTEEN

"Will there be anything else, Mr. Stapleton?"

I smile at Nancy, my housekeeper, and shake my head as I look around the spotless apartment. The floor is so clean I can see my reflection in it.

"No, that's it. You've done a fabulous job, as per usual. Say hi to Martin for me."

She nods and gathers her things and heads for the door, stopping long enough to lean down and pat Cat when he appears out of nowhere. Satisfied, he strolls over to the sofa and jumps up, making himself comfortable.

"Have a good night, Mr. Stapleton."

"Thanks, Nancy. You too."

After she's gone, I head to the kitchen to get everything ready. I may have exaggerated my cooking abilities, but I wanted to impress her. Besides, how hard can it be to follow a recipe?

As it turns out, it's harder than I thought.

The chicken is burnt, my potatoes are raw, and the kitchen looks a mess. Sighing, I grab my phone and call King.

"Yeah?"

"I need a favor."

"Okay…"

"Can I borrow Soula for tonight?"

"You wanna borrow my housekeeper?" He lets out a low rumbling laugh. "Why?"

"I gave Winston the night off, and now the kitchen is a mess, the food is fucked, and Ellie will be here any minute—" The intercom sounds. "Fuck. She's here."

"Wow, this chick must really be something if you're going all out to impress her. Here's what you do. Don't let her near the kitchen. I'll organize Jaime to prepare something special. Sound like a plan?"

Jaime. Why didn't I think of that?

"Great. Thanks, King. I owe you one."

"There's four words I promise to make sure you regret saying," he chuckles.

I end the call and answer the intercom, instructing the doorman to send Ellie up, then I race down to the bedroom to change my shirt, which is covered in I don't even know what. I'm still buttoning up my shirt when the doorbell rings. I run to the door and open it. Ellie stands there, looking sexy in a short, red dress.

"Hey," I say, an unfamiliar feeling of uncertainty rushing through me.

Why the fuck am I so nervous?

It isn't like this is a stranger. She's Ellie, for God's sake. But that's just the thing. Every other woman in my life was just a fling. Their names and faces blur together in a string of memories that are accentuated by expensive dinners, shallow conversation, and the hollow feeling I got the morning after. I didn't get what I was looking for.

With Ellie, everything is different. When I'm with her, we can talk about anything and everything, and I feel like I spent my time on something worthy. When I'm with her, the conversation is fun, interesting, and deep. She just doesn't do shallow. She's a different kind of woman, and I'm not used to that. All I know is I need to do everything I can to not let her slip through my fingers.

"Come in," I say. She does, her mouth falling open.

"This place is incredible," she breathes.

"You're incredible," I murmur in response.

She blushes, which makes my body react. God, I love it when she goes all shy and innocent. She really is beautiful, the rosy hue to her cheeks making her big eyes seem even brighter.

"The whole top floor is yours?" she asks.

"Nothing but the best," I say.

"Then why am I here?" she jokes.

"Because you're amazing."

I don't like that she's making jokes at her own expense. She really is everything I ever thought I needed. And in that red dress ... wow.

"Can I pour you a glass of wine?" I ask, breaking the awkward silence my comment caused.

She nods and goes to follow me to the kitchen, but I stop her.

"No. It isn't safe in there."

"Oh?" She laughs. "The cooking going that well, huh?"

"Oh, it's going. Right into the trash." I wince. "I have a confession to make. I can't really cook. I just wanted to impress you."

"That's so cute." She grins. "That's the sweetest thing anyone has ever done for me."

"You wouldn't say that if you saw how I slaughtered that poor chicken," I mutter.

"I'm sure it isn't that bad," she offers. "I can help you tidy up, at least."

"Oh, it's bad." I reach out and tug her arm, stopping her

from going in there. "Lucky for us, Jaime will be coming to our rescue. And the mess is no problem. Nancy will clean it tomorrow."

"Of course you have a housekeeper." She giggles as I steer her out onto the balcony.

I duck into the kitchen to retrieve the wine and two glasses. I find her standing by the railing, taking in the view.

"Holy shit, this view is amazing."

"It sure is," I agree, but it's her I'm looking at, not the city.

Cat wanders outside to see what the commotion is. Ellie turns around, her eyes lighting up when she spots him.

"Oh, who's this little guy?" Ellie coos, her eyes glittering.

"Cat," I say.

"You named your cat, Cat?" she asks, lifting an eyebrow.

I nod and pull up my shoulders. "I thought it was fitting."

"Well, it *is* accurate," she says. "What are you going to name your kids? Boy and Girl?"

I shrug. "If it suits them, why not? At least it'll be easy to remember."

Cat purrs and rubs himself against her legs. I watch as the creature that won't look at me twice acts like Ellie is the one person he's always loved.

"I can safely say he's a traitor," I add.

Ellie giggles and picks him up. "Should we be worried about him jumping over the edge?"

"You should be more worried about getting cat hair all over your dress," I say, my eyes on her again. "He's afraid of heights."

"A cat that's afraid of heights?"

She scratches Cat behind the ears as we head back inside. The damn cat is getting so much attention it's making me jealous. Where are my chin rubs?

"You're right about the hair," she says when Cat jumps out

of her arms and resumes his position on the couch. It's like she's wearing a fur coat.

"I can give you a shirt to wear if you don't want to ruin your dress," I smirk.

"Thanks, but I think I'll be fine." She giggles.

Too fucking bad. The thought of her in one of my shirts, with those long, bare legs is driving me wild. I hunch over the counter to hide just how worked up that thought has made me, and it doesn't go unnoticed by Ellie.

"Are you okay?" She narrows her eyes playfully. "You look a little flushed."

The intercom rings, thank Christ, so I make a beeline for it. "Yes?"

"Mr. Stapleton, there is a waiter here with a food delivery?"

"Right, please send him up."

*L*ike everything Jaime makes, the food is incredible.

"Better than what you could do?" Ellie teases.

"A glance in the kitchen will answer that question," I grumble. "I'm not sure where I went wrong. I tried this recipe out on Piper last week and it worked fine."

"So, is there anything you do for yourself?" she teases.

I raise an eyebrow. "You'll just have to wait and see." She blushes, her gaze dropping. "I was raised by a nanny," I explain. "Growing up, I had everything done for me. Now I'm so busy, it's just easier to hire people to cook and clean. It's bad, I know, but it's how it's always been."

"Did your parents both work when you were little?"

I hesitate. "My dad worked all the time. Right up until he died, he was a machine. Most days, I barely saw him. Sometimes

I wonder if he wanted kids at all. I think he did it to make my mom happy."

"Did she work too?" Ellie asks.

I shake my head. "No, she passed away when I was three-years-old."

Ellie looks up at me, sorrow on her features. "I'm so sorry." I can hear the sympathy—no, empathy—in her voice. But it's not the same as what happened with her.

"Don't be. I don't remember her, not really. Sometimes, a certain perfume might take me back to a memory I can just barely grasp, but my life with the nanny, and my dad just being there to pay for everything he thought would make me happy, is all I know."

She nods, popping a piece of tomato into her mouth.

"How is your mom doing?" I ask.

"She's doing great. She's sleeping and eating, which means she started complaining about gaining weight again." Ellie shakes her head with a fond smile. I love the way she talks about her mom. "Which means she's happy."

"I'm glad to hear it."

She glances up at me. I can almost hear the thanks forming on her lips, but I shake my head. I don't want to hear it; it was my pleasure, and it's in the past. She seems to know I'm going to say something about her thanking me again, so instead, she smiles at me.

She's so far from me, sitting on the other side of the table. When I finish my food, I pick up my glass of wine and walk around the table, sitting next to her instead. She smiles at me, and I brush her hair off her shoulder.

"Thank you for coming," I say.

"Thank you for asking me to come."

I smile. "You're a tough one to get out on a date."

"I don't want you to get the wrong idea about me."

"Yeah?" I ask and cock a smile. "And what idea is that?"

"That I might like you."

She speaks with such honesty and vulnerability, like she's afraid I'm going to hurt her. It makes me want to pull her into my arms and promise her I won't hurt her. She blinks at me, and I notice how long her lashes are. Her cheeks are red, her lips are perfect and so damn close. I can't help myself. I close the distance and press my mouth against hers, tasting her lips. She leans into the kiss, groaning as I run my hand over her bare shoulder, then down her back.

God, I want her.

My cock is already hard just thinking about being with her. The wine only fuels my need for her, and everything about Ellie is an aphrodisiac. Leaning forward, I bracket her face with my hands and kiss her, sliding my tongue into her mouth. She moans softly as I move my hand from her cheek to her shoulder and tug down the sleeve so that her shoulder is completely bare.

I move my lips from hers and kiss my way her down her jaw, down her neck, and then across her shoulder. She tilts her head, a sigh escaping her lips as my hand drifts to her breasts. She turns so I'm facing her and places her hand on my thigh.

My fingers travel under her skirt, and she tilts her hips forward a little, giving me access. My fingers brush against her panties, and she shivers. My cock hardens, straining against my pants, begging to get out. Biting her lip, she keeps her eyes on me as she reaches down. Her fingers are on fire when she touches me. I grunt as she lowers the zipper of my pants and reaches inside, gripping hold of my cock. She rubs her hands up and down my shaft.

Holy fuck.

I rub her through her panties, the dampness of the material turning me on.

"I want you," I murmur against her lips, her scent rising up to me.

"Then take me."

She doesn't have to tell me again.

I get to my feet, pulling her up with me, pushing my erection against her wetness as I kiss her roughly on the lips.

I grind against her a few times, my hands around her waist, before I carry her to my bedroom. Laying her on the bed, I kiss her again, my hands sliding along her thighs, creeping under the skirt of her dress. I ride my hands up until I find the waistband of her panties and slowly roll them down her thighs, as if I'm unwrapping a present. She leans back as I pull them off, and I groan as her scent engulfs me, my cock throbbing. I want her so bad, but I'm going to take my time.

I gently nudge her back on the mattress and lean down, pushing her red skirt up until it bunches around her hips. Her pussy looks incredible as she opens her legs for me. I dive in, closing my mouth over her smooth slit and lick her, my tongue sliding along her entrance. She moans as I dig deeper, flicking my tongue over her clit. I suck, my hands holding her hips still as she writhes beneath me. Her scent is driving me crazy. I feel dizzy, like I've had too much to drink, but I know it's because the blood flooded to my cock.

I push two fingers into her pussy, and she cries out, her body clamping down around my fingers. Slowly, I finger fuck her while I run my tongue along her slit, relishing the way her hips rise to meet my mouth and hand with every thrust. I bring her closer and closer to an orgasm. She trembles, her whole body shivering as she comes on my fingers. Her body tenses as she comes, her hips bucking forward to push hard against my mouth. Her pussy contracts around my fingers one last time as she cries out. Her fingers slide through my hair as she pulls me closer, as if she's begging me to go deeper. She gasps, her body going limp as she lays back on my bed, out of breath.

"That was..." She shakes her head, as if words can't describe how she's feeling.

"Just the beginning," I assure her.

She giggles as I sit her up on the edge of the bed. I reach behind, my hands fumbling with the zipper to her dress. Eventually, I pull it down. She stands as I peel it down her body, then she steps out of it and kicks it aside. Reaching for my shirt, she unbuttons it one by one, until her hands are running over my smooth, bare chest. She pushes the shirt off my shoulders, and it joins her dress on the floor.

I let her unbuckle my pants, then I slide them off and stand in front of her, but not before I grab a condom from the pocket. Her eyes narrow as she smiles.

"Presumptuous much?"

"I prefer to call it prepared," I murmur, rolling it onto my length.

She takes me in her hands, her fingers like silk when she touches my shaft, even through the thin barrier of the rubber. I groan and kiss her head, then I lay her back, so I'm on top of her. She sighs, her long legs wrapping around my waist. There's nowhere else for me to go but inside her. I push into her wetness, her body yielding as it caves around me. I groan as I slide into her as far as I can go. She moans as she grips my shoulders, her fingers digging deep into my skin. Her eyes meet mine as her lips part, and I press my mouth against hers.

She arches her back, her hips meeting mine with every thrust. Her body is heaven beneath mine, like we are made for each other. I dip my head and close my mouth around one of her nipples until it's stiff against my tongue, and then the other, while I slowly slide in and out of her. She moans, curling her legs around my waist, pulling me in deeper.

"More," she whispers.

I oblige, bucking my hips harder and faster, giving her what she wants. She cries out, the sight of her about to climax almost enough for me to lose my load, but I'm not ready to let go just yet. When I slide out of her, she opens her eyes, surprised, until I roll onto my back and motion for her to climb on. Her eyes shine as she lifts herself over me, and she straddles my hips.

I grunt, the sight of her firm breasts bouncing as she rides me almost enough to push me over the edge. She braces herself, placing her hands on my chest.

God, she feels fucking fantastic.

I stare at her body, committing it all to memory, to replay those nights when I'm alone and can't get her off my mind. She rocks back and forth faster and harder, riding my cock. I grab her hips, burying myself deeper inside her. Her face twists in a sexy expression that can only mean she's close to yet another orgasm. My balls tighten, and my body coils because I'm ready to release too.

She rocks harder and faster, moaning loudly, crying out with every thrust. I watch her face as her eyes close. Her brows knit together, and she bites her lower lip, that sight alone pushing me over the edge.

"Fuck," I groan, shoving my cock as deep into her as I can.

I gasp as I release, my body jerking forward. Her pussy closes around me, her muscles contracting, until they eventually let go. She collapses on my chest, breathing hard, riding the wave of pleasure that washes over the both of us again and again.

Finally, she sighs and glances up at me through hooded eyes. I stroke her hair and smile up at her. She rolls off me, and we both take a moment just to catch our breath. She shifts a little closer and puts her head on my chest, and my heart beats against her cheek. She looks past me, out the window, and the city is stretched at our feet like an ocean of lights. Her breath catches in her throat.

"Is this how you fall asleep every night?" she asks.

I nod. "It's even more beautiful with you here."

She turns her face to me, and I kiss her again, this time, slowly and sensually. I pour everything I'm feeling for her, everything that's too early to say to her, into that kiss.

"I have to go," she whispers into the darkness.

"Stay."

She tilts her head up and kisses me. "I can't. My mom will worry."

I want her to throw caution to the wind and do what she wants without thinking of anyone else. But if she did, she wouldn't be Ellie; she wouldn't be the woman I'm falling in love with.

"Okay," I finally concede.

"I feel like the guy. We had sex, and now I'm leaving."

She bites her lip as she looks up at me. I chuckle and drop a kiss in her hair.

"It's fine, this is so much more than just sex."

She nods and rolls off the bed, walking to the bathroom. When she flicks on the light, I see her looking around. I stare at her perfect body, bathed in light, before she disappears around the corner.

"This bathroom is bigger than my bedroom at home," she announces.

I chuckle in the dark and wait for her to finish up. She flicks the lights off, before she gets dressed in the red dress that's driven me crazy.

"I wish you could stay," I say.

She nods. "Me too."

That's all I need to hear. I get up, pull on boxer shorts, and escort her to the door. Before she leaves, she kisses me.

"Thank you," she says.

"Thank *you*," I murmur, giving her one last kiss.

CHAPTER FOURTEEN

Over the next few days, I don't see as much of Jack as I'd like. Work is hectic preparing for the competition, which means I've been putting in extra hours. I haven't seen Jack at all at work and by the time I get home, I'm too exhausted to do anything.

I'm in the staffroom on my lunch break when Piper walks in.

"Hey. How's it going?" she asks, making herself a coffee.

"Great. Busy, but I'm loving it," I say.

She sits at the table next to me and takes a sip of her coffee.

"Fuck, that's good," she mutters. "I'll never understand people who don't drink coffee. I live on the stuff."

I hold back a smile. I'm really starting to like Piper. She's a lot like her brother, in that they have the same confident, easy-going nature. But where Jack likes to remain composed and in control, Piper is down to earth and approachable. The simple fact that she's sitting in the breakroom, having a coffee shows how different they are. Jack wouldn't even think of doing that, not when he could send someone out to fetch it for him from an upscale café.

We chat for a few more minutes, but then I get back to work. The floor is hectic today, so when I finally get my lunch break, it's almost three in the afternoon. I'm starving, but rather than waste it eating lunch, I slip away to the elevator and head for Jack's office. It's been a few days since I've seen him, and though we've been sharing text messages, it isn't the same.

Cindy isn't at her desk when I arrive, so I take the opportunity to sneak past and enter Jack's office. As I turn the handle, it hits me that I might be about to interrupt something important, but it's too late to back out now. I open the door enough to peek inside and breathe a sigh of relief when I see he's alone. He looks up from his desk with a frown, but it disappears when he sees me.

"This is a nice surprise," he murmurs, leaning back in his chair.

"I skipped my lunchbreak to see you," I tease.

Jack shakes his head. "Then you must be starving."

"Why do you think I'm here?" I say, sashaying over to his desk.

A low growl escapes his throat as he swivels his chair around to face me. He wraps his arms around my thighs and looks up at me as I lean down to kiss him.

"To interview for the position as my assistant?" he asks when I finally break the kiss.

"Guess again," I say with a giggle. "Besides, I'm happy where I am."

"That's a pity. You'd be around me all the time."

I bite my lip. That does sound good, but I stand my ground.

"No. I really like where I am."

"Are you sure? I can offer you a much better position..."

His eyes are filled with hunger, and I realize he isn't talking about the job anymore. Heat pools between my legs as he tugs my hand and pulls me closer to him.

"What position is that?" I ask. My voice has gone breathy.

"Let me show you." Jack stands up, kissing me hard against the lips.

"You have windows everywhere."

My eyes dart around. Nobody can see us, but the risk is still there. Jack leans over to his desk and presses a button on a remote. The windows become foggy, like bathroom glass, and I can't see through it anymore.

"Wow," I say, impressed.

"You should see what else I can do," he chuckles, kissing me roughly.

His hands slide down to my breasts, cupping them for just a second before he unbuttons the white shirt that is part of my uniform. He untucks it from my skirt and then reaches into the cups of my bra to free my breasts. Eyes firmly on me, he lowers his head and takes my nipple into his mouth, sucking on it until it's hard and erect. He swirls his tongue around it, sending a direct line to my aching pussy.

Fuck, I'm so wet.

"I missed you," he murmurs against my skin.

"I missed you too," I admit.

Much more than I ever excepted I would. He kisses his way back up to my mouth, slipping his tongue into between my lips. Slowly, he works my skirt up so that my panties are exposed.

"Should I be worried if this is the treatment your assistant receives?" I tease.

"That would only be if *you* were that assistant." His eyes gleam. "Cindy will be on her break for another half hour, you know."

"Too bad mine is almost over," I grin.

With a low rumble, he pushes my legs apart. He runs his fingernail along my slit, over the thin fabric of my panties. I groan, aching to feel him inside me, but I stay strong.

"I have to get back to work," I whisper.

Jack pauses, blinking at me. With one hand still firmly between my legs, cupping my sex, he reaches for the phone.

"Piper?"

My eyes widen. He's calling his *sister* while touching me like this?

"Tell Cameron I'm in a meeting with Ellie. She'll be down as soon as we're done." He puts the phone down and gives me a wicked smile. "There. Your schedule is clear for at least three orgasms."

"Okay," I say, a smile tugging at my lips. "I guess I can't argue with that."

I groan as he tugs my panties aside and slides a finger into me. I gasp and clench my thighs together, my arms wrapped tightly around him. I lean back against his desk, tilting one leg to give him more space to work with. He gently slides his fingers back and forth inside me while he thumbs my clit, his other hand on my stomach, keeping me from moving.

"You're driving me crazy," I whimper.

"Tell me what you want," he urges.

"I want to come," I moan.

He chuckles, alternating his focus between my entrance and my clit. Every movement of his fingers has me crying out in pleasure. I clutch at his hand, begging him to finish me off.

"Please," I groan.

He chuckles as he rubs my clit in fast, furious circles. I curl around his hand and pull myself upright, so my head is leaning against his chest. I cry out, doing my best to stay quiet as my orgasm crashes down on me, my whole body alive, like it's on fire.

"That's one down,"

It takes me a moment to realize what he means. He doesn't give me long to recover. I lift my head and kiss him deeply, our tongues clashing. Then out of nowhere, he spins me around so I'm facing his desk. His body presses against mine as he nuzzles my neck, his hands rolling over my ass. He squeezes my cheeks so hard I squeal. I turn back and watch his expression as his fingers delve awfully close to my back hole. I brace my hands on the desk, waiting in anticipation for whatever he plans to do to me.

God, everything with him is a thrill. He's a ripple in the pool of my sedated life. He makes me want to be impulsive. I want to surprise him and show him I have a wild side.

I shiver at the sound of his zipper lowering, then he tugs my panties down until they're around my knees. I hear the crinkle of a foil wrapper, then he pauses for a moment before his cock finds my entrance. I'm wet and ready, and when he pushes into me, I moan. I try to swallow my cries, but it's hard to stay quiet with him burying himself deep into my wetness.

He bucks his hips faster and faster, the button of his pants brushing against my ass with every thrust, and his hands grip my hips tightly. I moan, my cries in rhythm with his thrusting, his strokes coming hard and fast. My hands press against his desk as he pushes me closer to a second orgasm.

He leans against me, reaching around to palm my breasts. I groan and throw my head back as my legs turn to jelly. Pleasure unfurls inside of me as I gasp for breath, while my heart pounds in my chest.

"Two."

He slows his thrusts, letting me ride out the orgasm before he picks up the pace again. Gasping, I bend over his desk, struggling to keep up. Jack pulls out of me and shifts his chair closer, sitting back down. I look at him as he curls his finger at me, motioning for me to climb on.

A fire in my belly, I push up from the desk. My panties fall to my ankles, and I step out of them. He puts his hands on my hips as I climb onto his lap, straddling him, grinding myself against him. I sink onto his cock, and he groans. In the bright light of his office, his face is riddled with pleasure as I ride his cock. I rock my hips back and forth, his eyes filling with a hunger I've never seen before.

He wraps his arms around my waist and drags me down onto him, fucking him hard. My clit rubs against his shaft as I slide down on him, my body a trembling mess.

"Come for me," he mutters, the friction on my clit threatening to make me do just that. "You're so fucking beautiful when you come," he says in a hoarse voice.

I kiss him, relishing when he moans into my mouth. I rock harder and faster, sliding him as deep into me as I can handle.

"God," I gasp, crying out in pleasure.

My gasps become louder and more consistent as I near another orgasm. I work my clit against him, feeling his cock deep inside of me.

"I'm close," I whisper against his mouth, our lips fractions apart.

"Me too."

It only spurs me on. I *want* him to come inside of me. I can't think of anything I'd love more than feeling him pulsate inside of me, filling me up with thick dick until I can't take it anymore. He groans, and I feel him jerk inside of me. I sit down hard on him, so that he's buried all the way, and I orgasm.

We ride the wave of pleasure together, and it's incredible. I forget about everything. I forget he's my boss, that he paid my debt, how scared I am to give myself to him completely... None of it matters in this moment. It's just him and me, in his office. Nothing else matters. All I can think about is how right being with him feels. Eventually we come down from our high. I sigh, breathing hard as I look down at him.

"Three," he says breathlessly.

"You're unbelievable," I say.

"So I've been told, once or twice."

I lift myself off his cock and stand. My legs feel like jelly, but I clean myself up, then pull on my panties. The last thing I want to do is walk back out there, looking like I just fucked my boss in his office. Jack stands too, zipping up his pants. He smirks at me as I tuck in my shirt.

"That concludes our meeting for today," he says. "You're free to go back to work."

"Thank you for taking the time to see me," I tease.

"One last thing before you go." He grabs my hand and pulls me into his arms. "Come out with me tonight," he says. "On a real date."

"What were the last two dates?" I laugh. "Practice runs?"

He shrugs, looking embarrassed. "I was holding back. I didn't want to overwhelm you with too much too soon."

I smile at him. "I can handle anything you throw at me, Jack."

"Then I'll go all out." His eyes twinkle, and I can still feel his cock pulsing inside of me. I shiver.

"Fine. I'll take it all."

Jack's face splits in a grin. "I have no doubt you will. I'll pick you up at seven."

I nod and walk toward the door. When I let myself out, Cindy still isn't there, which I'm relieved about. It would be kind of awkward if she heard any of that.

⸙

It's just after seven when Jack arrives at my house. I quickly go outside before Mom can start sharing any embarrassing childhood stories. He whistles softly as I walk down the path toward him. He's standing beside his expensive looking car that I'm guessing is worth more than our house.

"I'm surprised you don't have a driver," I tease.

"I do. Victor. I gave him the night off, just in case we get too ... intimate." His gaze burns through me. I shiver under the intensity of his stare. "You look fucking incredible, as usual," he mutters. "You just about blow my mind every time I see you." I look down and laugh, not sure how to handle so many compliments. "I don't think you realize how beautiful you are," he adds when I don't reply.

He opens the car door for me, and I slide in, buckling in my belt. I wonder what he has in store for us tonight. Every date feels impossible to top, but somehow he keeps on managing it. We drive a short distance before he turns into what looks like a parking lot. It has a helipad, and a helicopter is waiting.

"Are we going in that?" I ask.

Jack nods. "I hope you aren't afraid of flying."

I shake my head. I'm afraid of falling, but it isn't the same thing. He leads me to the helicopter, and I expect to be introduced to our pilot, but to my shock, Jack climbs into the driver's seat. I laugh. I should be surprised, but nothing Jack does shocks me anymore.

"Here."

I take the headset he offers me and slide it on.

"I've never been in a helicopter before," I say through the mic at my mouth. "This is amazing!"

Jack laughs. "I thought you might like it."

"You know, it takes a lot more than hiring a helicopter to impress me," I tease.

"I didn't hire it. I own it."

I gawk at him. Who the hell owns a helicopter?

Well, except maybe for Christian Grey, but fictional characters don't count.

We fly up and over the city, and the view is stunning. The sun is starting to set, and the horizon looks like it's on fire, a golden line that divides the Earth and the sky. We don't go far, before the helicopter circles back, landing on a roof. It takes me a minute to realize we're on top of his casino. I didn't know there was a helipad up here.

He kisses me and leads me around the side, to a rooftop garden—another thing I never knew existed. Once again, he's gone to so much trouble to try to impress me. It's absolutely beautiful up here, with plants, trees, and flowers in hanging pots. In the middle of it all is a picnic, laid out on a crisp blanket, with every gourmet food I could imagine, and enough wine to make me very tipsy.

"This is amazing," I whisper.

"A picnic under the stars."

We sit together on the blanket. He motions for me to move closer. I do, so I'm lying in his arms. I smile up at him and nuzzle against his chest. This is by far the most romantic thing anyone has ever done for me—then again, everything Jack does is romantic. I swallow hard, pushing my emotions away. I'm *not* going to ruin the most romantic date I've ever been on by crying.

"This really is incredible," I say again while we eat.

"You said that already, like a thousand times."

I shrug. "Sorry, but I'm used to guys thinking a DVD and popcorn is going all out to impress me. You take things to a whole other level, even when you were trying to hide the fact that you're super rich."

He pulls up his shoulder. "You deserve to be made to feel special."

I smile at him. I feel incredibly special.

"Are you and Piper close?" I ask.

Jack blinks, surprised by my question, but then he nods.

"Yeah, we are. We have our moments, like all siblings do,

but at the end of the day, I'd do anything to protect her. She and my friends are literally the only family I have left. I guess that's the beauty of growing up, huh?"

"What do you mean?" I ask.

"You get to choose the people you want to spend time with."

"Like me?" I muster up the courage to ask.

"Especially you," Jack reaches over to caress my face.

My heart flutters under the warmth of his gaze. I feel the same way, but it's far too early to talk about feelings. Even admitting to myself that I'm falling for him is too much, but when I look at him, there's something there that's so very different from anything I've felt before.

Is that what this is; am I falling in love with Jack?

After we finish eating, we lay on the blanket, wrapped in each other's arms. Jack holds my hand, fingers entwined, our palms pressed tightly against one another. I gaze off into the distance, taking in the stars. It's rare the night is so clear that you can see for miles. From this angle, the sky looks like a bowl of diamonds have been poured out; a mirror image of the city lights below.

He tilts his head toward me and kisses me. It's his usual lust-filled kiss. This one is slower, like there's meaning behind it he can't yet put into words. I feel it too, and it both scares me and excites the hell out of me.

"So, I have a thing tomorrow night," he murmurs.

"Yeah?"

He nods. "Would you like to come with me and meet some of my friends?"

I hesitate for a moment. Meeting friends means I'm on the radar. I might not have known who he was in the beginning, but

I get the feeling Jack Stapleton having a girlfriend is a huge deal. Maybe meeting his friends won't be that bad, but am I ready to be thrust into the spotlight as his?

The way I'm starting to feel for him, I'm not sure I have a choice.

"I'd love to," I say with a smile.

CHAPTER FIFTEEN

"So where are we going?"

Jack Shrugs. "Some new club one of my friends keeps raving on about. All I really care about is that I'll be there with you."

I stare at Jack when Victor pulls up outside Roxy. This isn't just any club. It's probably the most exclusive club in Vegas. Everyone who is rich, famous, or part of the in-crowd hangs out here. I only know because Bea won't shut up about it. She's never tried bringing me here. People like us don't even bother aiming that high. Even the line stretching around the corner is full of people of higher status than me.

Not tonight, though. Tonight, everything is different because I'm with Jack.

Jack takes my hand, his warm fingers interlinking with mine as we get out of the car. Cameras flash around us, and I'm very aware of how we look together.

Like a couple.

I glance at him, my heart racing. Is that what we are?

We reach the door, Jack shakes the bouncer's hand, like

they're old friends, and we're escorted inside. I look around, amazed. The club is incredible. Dim lights create the mood, sultry music sweeps around the dancers who move their bodies to the beat like a giant pulse, and the atmosphere is accentuated with everyone having fun.

"Come on," Jack murmurs.

He leads me up a spiral staircase that leads us to the second floor. We walk into an area that's blocked off with a red chord. A VIP area. Of course. I narrow my eyes at him playfully. Does everything come easily for him? I can't imagine he's had to struggle for anything in his life. It makes me wonder what he sees in me and whether I'm enough for him. For now, sure, but what about in the long run?

Am I enough to compete with the level of luxury he's so accustomed to?

I shake off the negative feelings because I'm not going to focus on that right now. I'm here to have fun. Jack touches my elbow lightly and leans in so that I can hear him over the music.

"Are you okay?" Concern creases his eyebrows. "You look ... sad."

"More overwhelmed. I'm pretty sure I've seen more celebrities in here than at the MTV awards."

Jack chuckles and puts his arm around my waist, pulling me closer.

"It must be nice to get what you want all the time," I can't help adding.

"Yeah, it is nice, I guess, but I don't care about that shit. I care about working for what I want," he replies. "The reward is bigger when I feel like I've earned it."

It's the answer I needed to hear, and it sets me at ease.

"My friends can be a handful," Jack warns as we walk into the room.

"If I can handle you, I'm sure they'll be no trouble." I grin.

"Jackie boy!" One of the three men lounging in the over-sized leather armchairs gets to his feet and embraces Jack.

"Ace, fuck, calm down." Jack chuckles.

I smile, feeling nervous. First impression is they *do* seem louder than Jack. All three of them look slick, rich, and act like they know they're in charge. They're all ridiculously attractive too, which makes me wonder are all young rich people this attractive?

Jack clutches my hand and nudges me closer to him, as if he senses I'm nervous. The guys all look me up and down, and I feel self-conscious. The attention of all of them at the same time, when there is so much in their eyes, makes me unsure of myself.

"This is Ace, King, and Asher," Jack says. "Guys, this is Ellie."

I blurt out a giggle. "Ace, Jack, King...what are you, a deck of cards?"

"Maybe we should start calling Asher Joker," King muses. "He is getting married, after all."

The guys bicker among themselves, while Jack turns his focus to me. I feel giddy inside; he's so intent on making sure I'm okay. I squeeze his hand to let him know I'm good, then we move to the couch and sit.

"Hey, everyone."

I look up and smile at Piper. I didn't know she was coming tonight, but I'm happy to see her. She's wearing a dress just as short and tight as mine, that probably cost a thousand times as much. She moves around the room, kissing everyone hello. I watch her, envious of her confidence. She's so comfortable in her skin, a concept which is foreign to me.

"Ellie! I'm so glad you're here." She throws her arms around me in a warm embrace like we're old friends. "I hate being the only girl," she whispers in my ear. "Jack sucks at gossiping."

"Piper," King's gaze burns through her. "I'd tell you how hot you look in that dress, but I wouldn't want your brother being a pussy about it."

Jack tenses beside me, but I'm too busy staring at Piper to pay him attention. Her glowing cheeks, the way her eyelashes flutter when King addresses her... Is something going on between her and King?

I shift my attention back to Jack and swallow a laugh. Judging by the death stare he's giving King, I doubt it. King's attention falls away from Piper and shifts onto the little waitress who's come in carrying glasses of what I'm guessing is whiskey.

"Macallan M?" Jack asks.

"Is there anything else worth drinking?" King retorts, taking one of the glasses.

Asher shakes his head when the waitress offers him one. He stares at his phone, deep in thought. I glance at Jack and see he's noticed his friend's odd mood too.

"On no, I don't drink the strong stuff," I say when the waitress reaches me.

"Explains why you're with Jack," Ace cracks.

"Ellie can drink wine with me," Piper offers.

"Sounds great."

She smiles at the waitress. "Can we get a bottle of Musigny's Grand Cru, please."

I blink at her, no idea what she just ordered. When I drink wine that has a cork in it rather than a screw top, I consider myself fancy.

"You'll love it," she says as if she knows what I'm thinking.

She's right. I do love it.

I sip at my wine and listen to everyone talking. The more I drink, the less anxious I feel, but I'm also mindful of not getting drunk and making a fool of myself. When Jack disappears for a few minutes with King and Asher, I make an effort to talk more with Piper.

"You were right about the wine. It's amazing," I tell her.

"At that price, I should damn well hope so." She laughs. "What can I say? I have expensive tastes."

"Jack seems to have expensive taste too."

I mumble it more to myself than her, the doubt creeping back into my heart. Watching him here, talking with his friends, he fits right in; whereas I'm sure I stick out like a sore thumb.

"Jack knows what he wants. And apparently, that's you. Fuck company policy when you're the boss, hey?" She's only teasing, but her words make me panic.

"You're not going to get me fire, are you?" I ask.

Piper laughs. "Relax. Even if I wanted to, I don't have authority over Jack. Besides, you're good for him."

"I am?"

She nods. "He needs someone who'll challenge him."

Something in the way she looks at me tells me she's known about us for a while now.

"How long have you known?" I ask.

"He told me." She gives me a sly look. "But you should probably also know we have cameras in our elevators…"

"Shit," I breathe, my cheeks growing warm.

Piper laughs again. "Relax, Ellie. Your secret's safe with me."

Little by little, I do relax. I don't know if it's the music, or the wine, or the fact that I'm so far out of my comfort zone I might as well go with it, but I'm starting to really enjoy myself.

"So, Jack says the guys are a handful."

I turn the conversation to his friends, who are standing together with their whiskey glasses, laughing about something. Their left hands are tucked in their pockets, making them like carbon copies of each other.

"Handful is an understatement," Piper snorts. "They think a lot about themselves; they know they're the shit. They have more money than sense, and when they get together, that can be dangerous." Piper nods at King. "He's an up and coming rock star who'll flirt with anything with a pulse."

"Including you?"

Her eyes narrow slightly. "Trust me. With King, it's nothing. *You're* not even safe. Asher owns a casino just like Jack," she continues. "And Ace is a professional poker player, which means he moves in the same circles as the rest of the guys. The thing about them is as over the top as they can be, their friendship *always* comes first."

I love that Jack has a good network of friends; people have his back, and he has theirs. It helps reassure me that I'm right about him being a good guy.

"So, you and my brother, huh?" Piper drawls, a sly grin playing on her lips as she brings the subject of conversation back around to us. "It must be serious if he's bringing you out where the Ratzi can see you."

"Ratzi?"

"The paparazzi. The guys are like royalty around Vegas. Anything new is major gossip. I guarantee you'll be all over the papers tomorrow."

Panic fills me, but it isn't because I'm worried about the world knowing about us. It's the fact that I haven't introduced him to Mom yet. I was waiting for the right moment. What if that chance is taken away from me, and she finds out because that picture is plastered all over the media? I don't want her thinking that she wasn't important enough to be one of the first people to meet him. Piper mistakes my unease for fear over my relationship with Jack.

"Relax and enjoy it, Ellie. Jack doesn't just close his eyes and jump, but when he sets his heart on something, he'll do whatever it takes to make it happen."

Heat creeps back into my cheeks as my stomach twists. A new wave of anxiety threatens to push through the haze of alcohol that's been hiding away my fears, but I refuse to let it. Not tonight... Not when I'm having such a good time.

Jack looks over his shoulder at me and offers me a smile, and the way he looks at me makes me warm again, but not my cheeks this time. My sex tingles as I watch him watching me, then as if he knows what I'm thinking, he wanders over to me and offers me his hand. I stand, and he wraps an arm around my waist, tugging me close. A sigh escapes my lips when he kisses me.

If only we were alone...

"Dance with me?"

He doesn't wait for an answer. Instead, he pulls me against him and grinds against me to the music. I forget about the world around us, about his friends and sister who are probably watching, about my hopes and dreams and fears and uncertainties. I just enjoy myself, letting the music guide me, letting Jack move me around on the little dance floor we've made out of our VIP lounge. His friends and Piper are still around, but I don't care. If Jack can have everything that he wants, then I can too.

And right now, *this* is what I want.

The night draws to an end, and we say our goodbyes to Jack's friends.

I hug Piper, really happy that she was here. I'm enjoying the friendship that seems to be growing between us.

"It really was great seeing you," she says, echoing my thoughts. Her voice drops to a whisper. "And I wasn't lying when I said it's great seeing you with Jack."

"Thanks, Piper." I give her another squeeze, then I take Jack's hand and let him lead me outside.

We step out into the night, the crisp air feeling good against my bare shoulders. Breathing in a deep breath, I sway a little on my feet. I may or may not be a little tipsy. Jack curls his arm around my waist and kisses my cheek, a smirk twisting across his lips.

"Do you want to come home with me?" he asks.

God, I want to say yes.

I've been craving his closeness all night, but I hate leaving Mom alone. That, and I'm probably the teeniest bit drunk.

"On second thought, I should probably take you home."

A swell of appreciation rises in my chest. The fact that he could pick up on my feelings and say something like that means the world to me.

We drive back to my place. Jack insists on getting out and walking me to the door. Once we're there, he smiles at me and reaches for my hand, his other hand caressing my face. I sigh as he pulls me closer, so our mouths are only inches apart.

"Can I kiss you?" he asks.

I lean in, closing the gap between us in response. Our lips clash together, syncing as one. It's such a beautiful moment that I don't want it to end, but I know I need to go inside.

"Thanks for tonight," I say. "I had a great time."

"I'm glad you enjoyed yourself. I was just happy to have you with me."

"Do you want to come to Asher's wedding with me over the weekend?" he asks.

I look up at him and nod. "I'd love to. Maybe you could meet my Mom before we leave?"

He kisses me again, running his hands through my hair as his tongue curls around mine. After what feels like a lifetime, he reluctantly pulls away, and I almost change my mind about going home with him.

"I'd love to meet your mom. Good night, Ellie."

"Night, Jack."

My stomach does a little flip as I open the door and Jack walks back to his car. I wait until he drives off, before I lock the door behind me. I'm surprised to find Mom in the living room, watching TV.

"You're still up," I say.

She nods, and I walk to the couch, dropping myself next to her. The smell of the club still clings to my clothes and hair.

"You look nice," Mom says.

"Thanks." I look at the dress, smoothing it over my thighs with my hands. "Did you wait up for me?"

Mom shakes her head. "I had a feeling you were in good company. I wasn't worried." She nods at the TV. "I can't get enough of this show. Binge-watching is an omen."

I giggle. "It's on-trend, mom. You're like everyone else now."

"Imagine my elation."

We both laugh. She presses pause on the remote and raises her eyebrows at me.

"The guy in the car looks cute."

I innocently glance at my mom. "What guy?"

"The one you were kissing," my mom reminds me, a smile playing around her lips.

"Oh, that one." I lean over and kiss Mom on the cheek, unable to hide my happiness. "Night, Mom."

"As long as you're happy, sweetheart."

I nod. "I am."

And I really mean it. In this moment, everything feels perfect. I feel like I'm floating on air. I feel like Jack is my Prince Charming, and I just arrived home from the ball.

His sister likes me. His friends like me. Everything is as it should be.

I know the wine is going to wear off, and my fears will be back with a vengeance, but I refuse to let it ruin how I'm feeling in this moment.

Right now, all I want to think about is Jack.

CHAPTER SIXTEEN

"Ash? What's up?"

"Fuck, Man." His words slur into one, and I know instantly he's been drinking. "I'm not sure I can do this."

"Do what?"

"Get married."

Shit.

"How much have you had to drink?" I say with a nervous chuckle.

"Not enough."

"You're fucking getting married tomorrow, and that's it," I promise him. "Even if I have to drag you down the aisle myself. What's wrong with you? Are you and Lake—"

"Lake's amazing. She's incredible, the most wonderful woman I've ever met." God, he's crying now. "I love her so much, man."

"Then what's the fucking problem?" I say with a laugh.

Asher is silent for a moment. "What if I fuck it all up? Things are great the way they are. I love her, I really do, but I'm terrified marriage is going to change us."

"Every man who ever got married was terrified the night

before. It's a natural thing to have some doubts before making such a huge commitment," I say to him. Then I have an idea. "How about you stay at the hotel? I'll get the guys together, and we'll come over and take your mind off things."

"You'd do that for me?" God, more tears.

I smile into my cell. "We'd do anything for you, man."

❦

After I end the call with Asher, I call the other guys, who are only too happy to help out. I suspect Ace is just happy for a reason to party, but I let that slide. Just as I'm about to leave the office to go home and get ready, Piper steps in. Her eyes narrow.

"Where are you off to?" she asks.

I nod upward. "The penthouse. I said Ash could stay there tonight. He's having a meltdown. I'm heading home to shower and then back here to make sure he doesn't do anything stupid."

"I'll come too," Piper immediately replies.

I shrug. "Whatever. Come if you want."

❦

After I go home and shower, I swing past to pick Piper up, and we head back to the hotel.

"So, are we still pretending like you're not trying to find every excuse you can to hang out with my friends?" I ask her.

Piper's cheeks redden. "Stop trying to read into something that isn't there, Jack."

I shrug. "If you say so. Just so you know, though. I've made it well aware to my friends that if they so much as touch you, I'll castrate them."

"Charming," she replies, making a face at me.

We arrive back at the hotel. Piper disappears, saying she'll meet me up there, so I take the elevator alone up to the penthouse. Only I'm not alone because when the doors open, Ellie is standing there.

"Hey," she says, giving me a shy smile.

"Hey back at you," I murmur, stepping close to her.

I lean in close to kiss her, but she steps back, her eyes widening.

"Did you know your sister saw us kissing last time?" she hisses

I laugh. "And?"

"What if other people see us?"

I pull her into my arms, spin her around and dip her down, pressing my mouth against hers. I stand her back up, then turn around and wave at the camera.

"I say let them see."

Ellie lets out a breathless laugh. "What the hell has gotten into you?"

"I'm just sick of hiding how I feel about you. I want the world to know that I'm into you," I mutter, my voice thick with emotion. "I have to go see Ash. He's having a minor meltdown. Pre-wedding jitters," I explain. "But I'll pick you up at eleven tomorrow?"

Ellie smiles at me. "I can't wait."

Asher is a mess when I walk into the penthouse. He staggers over to me and throws his arms around my neck, swaying as he mumbles something incoherent in my ear. I take his hand to lead him over to the couch, and he starts dancing with me.

"Easy, buddy." I smirk.

I finally get him to the couch and sit him down; mainly because I don't trust him not to fall over on his ass. The last thing we need is a broken nose, or any other kind of injury Lake would no doubt blame us for. I wince as I lean too close to him because he smells like a distillery.

"How much have you had to drink?"

He laughs off my comment and reaches into his pocket, pulling out a flask.

"Not enough."

"Jesus, Ash, what the fuck is up with you?"

"I'm just enjoying my last night of freedom," he slurs. "Isn't that what I'm supposed to be doing?"

"Where's the party at?"

We both look up when King and Ace walk in. Asher throws his hands up and cheers. His voice wobbles, then he leans against the couch, looking like he might throw up. He mumbles something else and then lays down. A few minutes later, he's asleep.

King, Ace, and I exchange a look, while we try not to laugh.

"I feel like I should be recording this to use it against him at a later stage," Ace mutters.

"Be nice," I say to Ace. "He's our friend, and we're going to take care of him."

I roll him on his side, just in case he is sick, then throw a blanket over him. When I'm done, I pour myself a drink.

"Stop, Jack. I'm fine. I just needed to let loose," Asher argues as he scrubs his hand over his face to erase his drunken state. He stands and makes his way through the penthouse as the rest of us relax now that the fog is lifting from him.

"This is nice actually," Ace says. "The four of us guys, together, the night before one of us gets married."

I chuckle because as loud and mischievous as Ace can be, deep down he's probably the most nostalgic out of all of us. The door opens again, and Piper strolls in. Ace scowls at her, like his vision of the perfect bachelor party just burst.

"You're not a dude."

Piper snorts. "No kidding, asshat."

"No," King murmurs, looking her up and down. "You're in no way, shape, or form manly. Having said that, I have no problem with you being here."

"I bet you don't." Ace winks at him.

"Am I missing something?" I ask suspiciously.

"Just that King obviously wants to bone your sister." Ace explains, like he's speaking fact.

"Then it's a good thing King knows if he goes anywhere near her, I'll string his balls through that chandelier up there," I say, nodding to the ceiling.

"Settle down, Sia," King grumbles.

"Hello? I'm right here," Piper huffs, glowering at me.

"I'm just making sure King knows his place," I say, not taking my eyes off my friend.

"I know my place alright." King winks at me, which only makes my anger boil. "Relax, man. Your sister is off limits. Doesn't mean I can't let her know I think she's hot, though."

"Cigar, anyone?"

Asher passes the box around, not so discreetly trying to change the subject. I take one and light it up, breathing the smoke into my lungs. The mood shifts back to light and cheerful, but I keep my eye on King. I know his reputation, and I've seen the way my sister looks at him. Even if she won't admit it, there's something there.

Asher flops down onto the couch next to me and sighs. I draw my attention away from King and look at my friend. Fuck, he looks a mess.

"How are you feeling?" I ask him.

He makes a face. "Like a man about to get married and...."

He stops speaking and rubs his jaw, so I nod toward the balcony door.

"You wanna get some fresh air?"

"Please."

He nods, and we both stand and take our drinks outside. The other guys are too caught up in their own conversation to notice we've slipped away. Outside, I sit on one of the armchairs, while Asher leans against the balcony, taking in the view.

"I thought you pretty much lived here," he comments.

"I did, but I don't trust Cat not to throw himself off the balcony."

Asher looks at me. "Who the fuck is Cat?"

I laugh. "He's a stray I found hanging out back a few weeks back."

"You took in a stray cat?" Asher looks shocked. "Who are you and what have you done with my friend?"

"What can I say, the scrawny little thing grew on me. I still hate animals, though," I add. I get to my feet and join him against railing. "You sure you're okay, man? I've never seen you so quiet."

"Just thinking, I guess." We're both silent for a moment, lost in our own thoughts. Then Asher looks at me, a panicked look in his eyes. "What if I'm doing the wrong thing by getting married? What if it's too soon?"

"You love her, right?"

"Well yeah—"

"Then that's all that matters." I tap my finger against the railing, taking in my own words. "If she's the first person you think of when you wake up and the last before you go to sleep, then she's your soul mate. Don't let that go."

"Are we still talking about me and Lake?" he jokes.

I smile. "Am I that obvious?"

"Kind of, but thanks. You're right. I do know Lake is the one."

He pats me on the back and wanders back inside, leaving

me out there alone to ponder. The cool breeze blows in my hair as I listen to the sounds of the Vegas nightlife. Sirens. Voices. Car horns. It's all here. The only thing missing is the one thing I want with me most of all.

Pulling out my phone, I snap a picture of the stunning view and send it to Ellie. I wait a few minutes before calling her.

"Are you trying to make me jealous?" she teases.

"No. Just reminding you how much I miss you," I murmur. "I wish you were here with me right now."

"Me too," she whispers softly.

Maybe it's the alcohol kicking in, but I suddenly feel a rush of confidence and a strong need to tell her how I feel.

"I love you, you know," I say out of nowhere.

"Isn't that the kind of thing you should say in person?" she replies nervously.

"Probably, but I couldn't wait," I say. "I mean, what if I were to plunge off this balcony tonight. I'd die without you ever knowing—"

"Jack, don't you dare."

I wince because I probably could've phrased that a little better for the girl who recently lost her dad to suicide.

"I didn't mean I was going to jump," I'm hasty to assure her. "I just meant sometimes things happen that are beyond our control. If you feel something, you should make it known the moment you feel it, or it might be too late."

"Then I love you too," she whispers.

CHAPTER SEVENTEEN

I shouldn't be as nervous as I am. It's not *my* wedding, after all, but my stomach is tied up in knots, and I just can't seem to get my makeup right. I've taken it off and reapplied it again three times. I let out a growl and toss my mascara across the room, wincing when it hits the window.

"Honey," Mom calls from the living room. "There's someone at the door for you."

Shit, he's here already?

I'm nowhere near ready to leave yet.

I glance at the time, confused. He isn't supposed to be here for another hour. Maybe he got the time mixed up? Either way, I better find out what he wants before Mom embarrasses me.

God, another reason why I'm so nervous.

When he offered to pick me up and I agreed, I totally forgot that would mean introducing him to my mother. I love Mom, but I've never had a boyfriend serious enough for her to meet, so I have no idea how this is going to go down. Then again, if things are getting serious, she has to meet him eventually.

"Ellie?" Mom calls again.

"Coming," I mutter, tightly wrapping my robe around my waist.

I jog down the stairs and walk into the living room, but it isn't Jack standing in there. It's Victor, his driver. He's holding a large, flat box.

"Victor," I blink at him in surprise. "What are you doing here?"

"I've brought you a gift from Mr. Stapleton." He hands me the box. "You can take your time to get ready. I'll wait."

I blink at him. "You're taking me to the wedding?"

Victor nods.

"Okay," I say in a small voice.

I glance at Mom and then walk back upstairs to my room, feeling a little deflated that Jack's not taking me to the wedding. I glance down at the long, thin box with Chanel delicately printed across the front and wonder what's inside. Whatever it is, it's about to become the most expensive thing I own.

Sitting on my bed, I lift the lid off the box and gasp. Inside is the most beautiful dress I've ever seen. It's layers of silk chiffon with delicate diamond encrusted straps. I hold it up, unable to imagine myself in something so stunning. I don't often wear dresses, but this is something else and no doubt worth an absolute fortune.

I finish my makeup, getting it just right, and then I curl my hair, letting it cascade down my shoulders. My heart races as I pick up the dress and step into it.

"Mom?" I call out. "Can you help?"

"What is it, honey—" She stops in the doorway, her eyes wide. They brim with tears as she covers her mouth with her hand. "Oh, Ellie. You look beautiful." She walks over and carefully raises the zipper, then I walk over to the mirror, nervous about seeing how I look.

Mom wipes the tears from her eyes as I face my reflection.

Holy shit.

The dress looks like it was made for me, with a scooping neckline that makes my breasts look perfect. But it's the back that I can't stop staring at. It's daringly low, but the long layers of skirt give it the perfect balance of elegance and sophistication.

"You look stunning," Mom whispers, a new rush of tears flowing down her cheeks. "He must be serious about you if he's sending you gifts like this."

I smile. "I think he might be."

"So, when do I get to meet this special man?"

I blush as I slip into some black strappy heels and then lift up my shoulder nonchalantly.

"Soon," I promise.

"Well, I hope so. I'm getting more and more curious by the day as to who is making my daughter so happy."

I glance at the time. Shit. Where did that hour go?

"I have to go, or I'm going to be late." I kiss Mom on the cheek, then spritz a bit of perfume on my wrists, before grabbing my purse and heading downstairs.

"Ready, ma'am?" Victor asks when I walk into the living room.

"Ready," I nod.

Outside, Victor opens the car door for me, and I slide onto the leather backseat, arranging the layers of dress around me. Just as the car pulls off, my phone pings with a message.

Jack: I'm sorry I couldn't pick you up. Asher is having a meltdown.

I smile and text him back.

Me: Take care of Asher. I'll see you there x

I love that he's such a good friend willing to do whatever he needs to in order to help out a friend. Just like he helped me. My heart sings, like I've just realized how lucky I am to have him in my life.

The drive to the venue is a short one. Asher's casino *The Grandiose*. I think it's an odd choice, until Victor leads me to the elevators and up to the top of the building.

Another rooftop?

I'm starting to wonder if it's a rich people thing.

I step outside and gasp; it's simply stunning. Rows of chairs covered in pristine white cloth and wrapped with pink silk sashes are perfectly lined up, facing the most stunning arch, decorated with pink roses. Petals scatter the walkway where the bride will be soon be embarking toward her new life with Asher. The stunning Vegas backdrop makes it all the more special.

A few of the guests are already here. They stand together in groups. It's not hard to tell that these people all come from a lot of money. They all look polished and dressed to kill. I'm nervous to join them because I don't know if I'll fit in. I certainly look the part, but I don't come from the same background. I'm different.

Someone waves at me, and it takes me a moment to recognize Piper. Relief washes through me as I walk over to her.

Finally, someone I know.

Piper looks stunning, even more than usual. Her hair is twisted into an elegant updo, and her makeup looks flawless. She's wearing a lilac sleeveless dress with lace cap sleeves and matching lilac shoes.

"You look incredible," she says after hugging me. "I think you even outshine me."

"Thanks," I bite my lip, looking down at the dress. "Jack sent it over."

"He has good taste," Piper grins. "And I'm not talking about the dress; God knows he didn't choose it." She takes my hand. "Come on. Let's find our seats."

We sit together. I feel a rush of disappointment that as the best man, Jack won't be with me. My eyes fall on him, and my breath catches. He looks amazing. He stands at the front in deep conversation with Asher. When he looks my way, I smile at him. Desire fills his eyes as he stares at me, like he can't look away. He mouths something to me:

You look beautiful.

Biting my lip, I look down to hide my smile. Slowly, the seats fill up, and the murmur falls silent when the music starts. We all stand and turn to watch the bride walk down the aisle. A collective murmur rises when a dog trots down the aisle first—

a friendly-looking mut carrying a ring box in his mouth.

"Come on, Elvis," Asher calls.

But Elvis has other ideas. Everyone laughs hysterically as the dog runs through the crowds of people, ignoring Asher's growing agitation.

"Elvis, come here," he growls.

The dog's ears prick up. He looks up at Asher, bows his head, and makes his way down the aisle with a whimper. A collective aww fills the air as everyone feels sorry for the poor dog. Eventually Elvis stops in front of Jack, dropping the box in his hand. Jack makes a face as he holds up the drool-covered box, and everyone laughs. He opens the box with a look of disdain on his face and holds the rings out, ready for Asher and Lake.

Bridesmaids follow, wearing pastel tulle dresses and high heels, smiling as they walk to the front, scattering more rose petals as they walk.

Finally, the bride appears. Everyone turns back, and a hush falls over the crowd when she steps onto the carpet. She looks breathtaking, holding her father's arm. She's wearing a dress so perfect, it looks like it was designed for her especially. I don't know Asher that well, or Lake, for that matter, but I have a lump in my throat when they take their hands. As beautiful as it is to watch, tears sting my eyes when her father flips her veil back and kisses her on the cheek.

It hits me like a freight train that I'll never get that moment. My father will never be able to walk me down the aisle, toward my future husband. A single tear trickles down my cheek as I realize how much I miss him.

I hate him for everything he did, for leaving us, but God do I miss him.

When the celebrant announces them husband and wife, a cheer erupts in the crowd. Everyone is happy, including me, but I'm not staring at the couple like everyone else is. I'm looking at Jack. He stands next to Asher, looking sexy in his tux. And his eyes are on me.

Piper nudges me. "You like him, don't you?"

I nod, swallowing the lump in my throat. "I really do."

"He likes you too."

I glance back at Jack, my heart pounding. Because right here in this moment, there is no doubt in my mind that I love him. Maybe it's the wedding, or the half a glass of champagne I've had, but I so badly want to tell him how much he means to me.

When the ceremony is over, and the confetti has been thrown, congratulations have been offered, Jack finally has a chance to sneak away and find me. I'm shy when he looks me up and down with eyes filled with equal parts affection and lust.

"You look amazing." His voice is low and husky.

"You do too," I say, my cheeks warm.

"God, it's torture standing up there knowing you're within reach, and I can't get to you." He wraps his arms around my waist and cups my cheeks, then he plants a quick kiss on my lips. "I'm sorry I haven't been able to get to you until now. It's been crazy."

I shake my head. "It's okay. I've been hanging out with Piper. I like her a lot."

"So long as you don't like her more than me."

"Not possible."

Before Jack can reply, he's summoned to take photos.

"I have to go," he says, looking annoyed. "But I'll find you again when we're done."

"I'll be waiting."

He grins and plants another kiss on my mouth before he walks away. I wait for Piper to finish her conversation, before I join her again.

"Come on," Piper says, linking her arm through mine. "I have it on good authority they're serving very expensive champagne while we wait for the photos to be taken."

I follow her to a table that's laid out with delicate crystal flutes, and we each take a glass.

"Piper, darling, is that you?" a boisterous woman cries out.

"Oh, God," Piper murmurs. "If I'm not done with this conversation in ten minutes, come save me." She plasters a smile on her face. "Mrs. Keller, it's *so* good to see you!"

I chuckle and step aside, holding my drink in my hand. When Piper talks, I feel a little self-conscious and out of place. She's my shield, when I'm with her I feel like I don't stand out so much.

I spot King and Ace, standing a few feet away, drinking whiskey. They have their backs to me, talking about something. I decide to join them. I only met them once, but it's better than not knowing anyone at all. When I approach them, I stop, overhearing my name. My heart pounds. I shouldn't be listening, but I can't help myself.

"You really think Jack isn't serious about Ellie?"

"Jack's never fucking serious about anyone."

"But he's brought her to a wedding," King argues. "That's gotta mean they're screwing at least, which means I win."

"No, the deal was he has to fall in love with her, so until I hear 'I love you' utter from his own lips, I'm keeping my cash to myself, thanks."

My stomach drops as they laugh, their voices fading as they wander off. Stepping back, I touch the back of my neck. I'm cold and clammy, but I feel like my skin is on fire.

Is that what I am, just some stupid bet?

I have to get out of here.

I rush for the door, desperate to get out of here before the tears fall. I know it's pathetic, but I can't stay, not after this. I should have known Jack was too good to be true.

I've just been too busy fooling myself into believing he wasn't.

CHAPTER EIGHTEEN

The photos are fucking taking forever, and my mouth stings from smiling so much, but Asher and his new bride look radiant and happy, and that's all that matters. After the meltdown he had earlier, I'm just glad we made it here at all.

Finally, after what feels like hours, we're done.

"Can I go and mingle now?" I ask Asher. "Am I relieved of my duties?"

He laughs and claps me on the back. "Sure. Thanks, man. For everything."

"Anytime." I smile at Asher. "You guys are perfect together. Just do me a favor and don't fuck it up."

Asher winks at me. "I won't if you won't."

I laugh. Ellie is the best thing in my life right now. I sure as hell don't plan on messing it up. Turning around, I search the crowd again for her, but I can't see her anywhere. I spy Piper talking to Asher's Mom. She gives me a pleading look, and I laugh and wander over to her.

"Sorry, Mrs. Keller, mind if I borrow my sister?"

"Certainly, Jack. It was a lovely wedding, wasn't it? Oh, Sandy, I need to speak with you about the committee meeting next week." Mrs. Keller races off after her friend, while Piper leans against me, feigning relief.

"Thank fuck for that," she hisses. "That woman could talk the stripes off a zebra."

I chuckle. "Hey, have you seen Ellie?"

Piper's expression changes to a puzzled one.

"Yeah, now that you mention it. She was walking over to the guys, and the next thing I know, she was bolting for the elevator." She shakes her head, confused. "Before that, we were having a great time."

Why would she just leave like that? I check my phone for a text or a call, but there's nothing.

"Maybe you should ask your two knucklehead friends."

"What do you mean?"

Piper shrugs. "I was too far away to hear anything, but it looked like she ran immediately after overhearing something they said?" She shrugs again. "I don't know; maybe I'm wrong."

I groan because knowing those two guys, she's probably right.

"Thanks, Pipe."

King and Ace are deep in conversation when I walk over to join them. They abruptly stop talking as soon as they notice me. Narrowing my eyes, I look from one to the other.

"Okay, fess up. What's going on?"

King shuffles on his feet, while Ace looks at the ground.

"We just want to know who won," King mumbles.

"Won what?" I ask, confused.

"The bet," Ace sighs. "Are you and Ellie ... you know?"

I curse under my breath. "Were you talking about that a few minutes ago?"

"Yeah, but—"

"Fuck," I hiss.

She must've heard them talking about their bet, and now she thinks I'm involved.

Shit. This is bad.

"I have to go."

I stalk toward the door, the only thing on my mind is finding Ellie, so I can make this right. I try calling her cell, but she doesn't answer. Outside, I scan the streets, looking for her, but she's nowhere in sight. I see Victor waiting by my car and run over to him.

"Have you seen Ellie?"

He nods. "She came out, looking upset. I offered to drive her wherever she was going, but she said no." He pauses. "She said she wanted nothing to do with you, Mr. Stapleton."

Fuck.

"Go home, Victor," I tell him. "I'll take my car."

❦

*B*anging on the front door of Ellie's house, I pray that I'm not too late. I don't even know what I'm gonna say when I see her. I just hope she believes that I had nothing to do with the guys and their stupid bet. My heart races when the doorknob turns, but it isn't Ellie.

It's her Mom.

"Hi, Mrs. Masters, I'm..." I shake my head, Ellie the only thing on my mind right now. Introductions can wait. "I need to talk to Ellie. Is she here?"

Her mother shakes her head. "I thought she was with you."

"If everything works out right, she will be," I say. "I just need to talk to her."

"Have you tried Bea's place?"

Bea. Of course.

"Thank you," I call out, already running back to my car.

I drive through the streets toward Bea's apartment, breaking every traffic rule along the way. I don't care — I'll pay the fines. The only thing that matters now is reaching Ellie. I need to explain everything to her before she thinks I'm the world's biggest asshole.

I pound on Bea's door over and over. I know someone's in there. I can hear voices on the other side. I'll stay here all night if I have to, until I talk to her. Finally, the door opens, revealing a very pissed looking Bea.

"Will you fuck off?" she hisses.

"No. I need to talk to Ellie."

"The hell you do," Bea says and folds her arms over her chest. "What makes you think she wants to see you? I told you what would happen if you hurt her—"

"I know it looks bad, but I promise it's all a misunderstanding," I cut in.

Bea lets out a sarcastic laugh. "Said every dipshit asshole in the world."

I rake my hand through my hair. "Please, just let me talk to her."

Bea narrows her eyes at me. For a second I think she's going to slam the door in my face, but then I hear Ellie's soft voice in the background.

"Let him in."

Bea glares for a moment longer, then she steps aside. I walk inside to find Ellie on the couch, her feet tucked under her, her high heels on the floor. The look in her eyes reminds me of that first night we met. Scared. Alone. Angry.

"Please, hear me out," I beg. "Ten minutes, then I'll leave if you want me to."

Ellie hesitates and glances at Bea, who shrugs.

"Okay," she finally says. "But not in here."

She stands from the couch, holding her dress loosely in one hand so that it doesn't drag on the floor now that she's on bare feet. She comes to me, and we step out of the apartment.

"I had nothing to do with the bet," I say.

"Why should I believe you?" she asks, and there's pain in her voice. "How do I know I wasn't just a bet, a game to you?"

"Because my friends are assholes. I don't think you're a game, Ellie. You're different than anyone I've ever met before. I would never do something so insensitive, and I sure as shit would never do something to screw things up between us. Not when I'm in love with you. Not when you're everything I want."

For a moment, she looks like she's going to cry, but she doesn't. She manages to keep herself composed.

"So, your friends bet on you sleeping with me?" she clarifies.

I nod. "Because I don't usually fall for someone the way I fell for you. They find that amusing. And trust me, I'll take care of them, but please don't let this come between us."

She hesitates, but then she nods.

"I'm sorry I hurt you," I say.

"I'm sorry I ran away."

I take her hand, squeezing it tightly. "So, you believe me?"

Ellie nods, and I sigh, releasing the breath I didn't even know I was holding onto.

Thank fuck for that. I don't know what I would've done if she didn't.

"What about the wedding?" she asks in a small voice. "I feel so bad for leaving."

"It was pretty much over anyway. Hey, do you want to go for a walk? It will be nice to slow down and clear our heads a little."

Ellie chuckles. "Slow down? You realize we're in Vegas, right?"

I shrug, touching her cheek. "It isn't where you are; it's who you're with."

She steps into the apartment to get her shoes while I wait for her outside. Bea hugs Ellie goodbye before she glares daggers at me.

"If you hurt her..."

"I know. There'll be hell to pay," I cut in. "But I won't hurt her."

Bea nods, satisfied. I leave my car for Victor to collect later and slide my hand around Ellie's waist. We walk in silence, both lost in our own thoughts. As we near the strip, the noise and atmosphere kicks up a notch. There really is no place like Vegas, especially at night. It's crazy how I made a life here. I have everything I could want. A hotel, a casino, my sister and friends who'd do anything for me—even unintentionally nearly mess everything up. But all that means nothing without Ellie by my side.

I only realize how far we've walked when we wind up in front of my apartment building.

"Well, would you look at that," I say, looking up at the building towering above us. "Since we're here, can I convince you to come up?"

Ellie smiles, her bottom lip catching in her teeth. "You can."

I look at her, and she's the most incredibly beautiful woman I've ever seen. Not only because she has a natural beauty, but because she's such a pure, wonderful person. She's changed my life completely.

"What?" Ellie asks.

"What do you mean what?"

"You're looking at me like that."

"Like what?"

"Like you want to kiss me."

"Well," I say and close the distance between us. "Maybe it's because I do want to kiss you."

My lips nuzzle against hers, and she melts against me. I sigh; there's no doubt in my mind that she's the one. When I'm with her, everything falls away. The world becomes perfect. When I'm with Ellie, I'm home.

Taking her hand, we walk into my apartment building and toward the elevators. As soon as the doors slide closed behind us, I kiss her again, this time with need, an urgency to feel her close to me. She wraps her arms around my neck, pressing the length of her body against mine, and I slide my tongue into her mouth, the friction causing her to moan.

The doors slide open, but I don't want to peel myself off her just yet, so we stumble back toward the door, our lips still connected. I fiddle with the keys and unlock my door, then I edge her into the penthouse and kick the door shut with my foot.

I kiss her again, my hands running down her bare back, and God I *want* her so fucking bad, but I break the kiss. She looks at me in surprise.

"I'm in love with you," I confess. "You know that, right?"

Color creeps across her cheeks as she flutters her eyelids. God, she's so sexy.

"I'm in love with you too," she whispers.

"Can we call us official now?"

She nods, her smile widening. "We can."

I lead her to my bedroom, the insatiable urge to be with her growing inside me. I want to undress her, I want to kiss her and touch her and taste her, and then I want to fuck her nice and slow so I can savor every second. I nudge her closer to me and kiss her again, tugging at the diamante strap on her shoulder. It slips off easily, and I pull the other one down too, revealing her perfectly rounded breasts. I reach behind her and cup her ass in my hands, squeezing and massaging it as I pull her tightly against me. My cock twitches at the sight of her glorious body. Just thinking about being inside her gets me hard.

Ellie smiles as she pushes my jacket down over my shoulders. I shrug it off and toss it on the floor, sending my shirt along with it, while her dress spills to the floor, pooling around her legs. Her hands move to my chest as I unbuckle my pants and push them off, along with my boxers.

I kiss her with such force that we tumble back onto the bed, tangled in each other's arms. She giggles as I run my hands over her body, pulling her closer to me, my cock pressing against her entrance.

"You're already wet for me," I growl.

Hell, she's wetter than wet.

Usually, I love teasing her, touching and exploring her. I love making her feel incredible, but right now, all I want is to be inside her. She spreads her legs, and I push into her. She cries out, and I let out a groan as my cock slides into her pussy. Her lips part, and her eyes glaze over as I roll her onto her back, peppering her with kisses. I slowly ease my cock out and slide it back in, repeating the action as she moans into my mouth. Fuck, she's amazing. I kiss her roughly, like I can't get enough of her. She gasps as I fuck her, my speed increasing with every thrust. My eyes locked on hers, I fuck her faster and harder, pushing her close to the edge.

This isn't fucking—it's making love. Because I love her.

I love her more than I ever thought it was possible to love a woman.

And she's mine now.

With a growl, I angle my cock, so it slides in deep. She cries out, her back arching as she comes on my cock. I growl, my dick jerking as I feel her wetness. I can feel the pleasure washing through her, the contraction of her pussy around my cock, and it's fucking amazing.

I kiss her again, swallowing her moans. We're connected together, so close that I don't know where I end and she begins. My balls tighten, and I bury myself deep inside of her with one final thrust when I come, pumping into her, coating her insides with my seed and marking her as mine.

All fucking mine.

She orgasms again at the same time as I do, her eyes closed, her lips parted. When my cock stops pulsating and the intense euphoria fades, I plant kisses all over her face, then pull out of her, roll over, and bring her against me. She rests her head on my chest, just where it belongs. The room has grown dark around us. Night has fallen, and we're still tangled together, just as we should be.

"Stay the night?" I murmur, nibbling at her ear.

She nods, and I close my eyes.

When I open my eyes again, the light that falls in through the window is bright, flooding the room. Somewhere during the night, I must have pulled sheets over us. We're both wrapped up in it now, Ellie's arm still thrown over my chest, her hair splayed over my shoulder.

I glance down at her, taking her in while she lays sleeping in my arms. She's fucking beautiful. I could stay like this forever and never get sick of looking at her. She flutters her eyes open and looks up at me, color creeping across her cheeks.

"Were you staring at me while I was sleeping?"

I nod. "Is that okay?" I ask, stroking my fingers down her cheek.

"Yes," she says, smiling at my touch. "I could do this every morning."

I smile at the idea. Slowly, we'll get there. Right now, I want to relish in what we are.

"Hey, what are you doing later?" I ask.

She thinks about it for a moment and then shakes her head.

"I don't think I have any plans."

"King has a show. Do you want to come with me, as my girlfriend? Piper will be there."

Ellie nods. "Okay, it sounds fun, but first, there's something else I want to do…"

She laughs as I roll her over and kiss her firmly on the lips, my hand cradling her face as our mouths explore each other.

"Oh yeah?" I mutter, nipping at her neck. "I can't wait to hear all about them…"

"I want you to meet my mother."

I roll her off me with a chuckle. "That's so not where I thought this was going." I look at her, my eyebrow raised, a smirk slowly spreading across my mouth. "Unless…"

"God, no," Ellie gasps, laughing. She leans over and hits me playfully on the arm. "I just meant I feel bad that I'm keeping her from you. Especially considering all you've done for us."

"And I'd do it all again, you know," I murmur. "In a second."

"I know you would." She smiles at me as I lean in to kiss her again. "That's part of why I love you so much."

"And I love you right back," I murmur.

My lips press against hers, and I find myself wanting her just as bad as I wanted her the first time we kissed. It's like I can't get enough of her. I want to hold her in my embrace all night and never let her go. She giggles as I kiss along her neck, licking her soft skin.

"Do you mind if I tell her?"

"Tell who what?" I ask, distracted by those how sweet her neck tastes.

"Mom. That you paid off the debt."

I pull away slightly, so I can see her expression. Honestly, I'm surprised she'd want to tell her about that, since she was so dead set against it in the first place.

"Whatever you want to do is fine with me," I say.

Ellie smiles at me, looking happier than I've seen her in a long time.

God, I love seeing her smile.

"Okay, then come over to my place for dinner tonight, before the show."

"I can't wait," I say kissing her again.

CHAPTER NINETEEN

nxiety pools in my stomach as I pace the living room. It's just after six, which means Jack will be arriving any moment to meet Mom. I move over to the window again and peek outside, something I seem to be doing every five seconds.

"Ellie, calm down." Mom chuckles as she walks over to me. She puts her hands on my shoulders, forcing me to look at her. "You're making me nervous, Ellie. What's with all the pacing?"

"I'm just..." I take a deep breath. "I just want you to like him."

"If you like him, there's a reason," she points out.

I nod, her words reassuring me.

Mom studies me closely. "This is more than like, though, isn't it?" Heat creeps into my cheeks. "I think you're in love with this man."

"I am," I whisper.

"Then I'm sure I'll love him too."

187

I check out the window again, the acid beginning to build up my throat. Maybe what I'm really nervous about is how Mom will react to the news that Jack paid off Dad's debt.

What if she reacts like I did?

"Can I talk to you about something?" I hedge, deciding this is a conversation I'd rather have with her before Jack gets here.

"You can talk to me about anything, darling," Mom says, sitting on the couch.

I walk over to the couch and sit next to her, my hands fidgeting in my lap. My heart races, and I can't make eye contact with her. I'm struggling to find the right words to tell her.

"Please, Ellie. You're making me nervous now." She frowns at me. "You're not pregnant, are you?"

I snort. "God no."

"Then what is it?"

"Jack paid our debt," I blurt out.

"He what?" She blinks at me, surprised.

"He paid Dad's debt," I repeat.

"Why would he do that?"

"He was worried about what Snake might do to us."

Mom stares at me for a moment, my words sinking in. "He did that for you?"

"He did it for us," I correct.

"Ellie, I don't know what to say," Mom whispers, shaking her head in wonder. "I hope you thanked him."

I blush. "I was angry at him at first. I went into his office and yelled at him. That's when he offered me the job." I hesitate. "I'm paying him back. Every last cent."

"Ellie—"

"I couldn't let him do it, Mom," I cut in. "It was too much. And while I'm so grateful he did it, I need to do what I can to make sure our relationship remains equal. I can't do that with this hanging over my head."

"I understand that."

"You do?" I whisper.

I was sure she wouldn't. I was sure she'd fight me on this one, but she isn't. She accepts why I need to do this.

"This boy..." she shakes her head. "He sounds like a keeper."

I let out a laugh. "I'm pretty sure he is."

The knock on the door makes me jump because I'm not expecting it. I race over to let him in, nervous about seeing him, even though it was only hours earlier I was lying in his arms. I open the door and smile at him. He looks sexy in his dress pants, a shirt, and a jacket—okay, so he looks the same as he does when he's at work, but still hot as hell.

"Hey," he says, kissing me softly on the lips.

"Hey back."

I kiss him, embarrassed that Mom's right there, watching us, but I get over it quickly. With a steadying breath, I take his hand and lead him over to Mom. My heart thumps wildly. I've never introduced a boyfriend to Mom before. I can't shake the feeling that this will be the first and last boyfriend of mine she meets.

I feel like this, right here, is the man I'm going to marry someday.

"This is Jack. Jack, this is my mom."

Jack puts out his hand, his usual charming self.

"It's lovely to meet you, Mrs. Masters."

"Oh please, call me Jill," Mom scoffs. "It's nice to meet you too, Jack."

Out of nowhere, she steps forward, wrapping her arms around Jack. He glances at me, surprised, then he hugs her back. She steps away, looking embarrassed. I smile because I can tell she loves him already.

"I'm sorry," she says. "It's just I can never thank you enough for what you did for us. You have no idea how much your gesture means to me."

"And you have no idea how much your daughter means to me," Jack replies sincerely.

I go weak at the knees, hearing him say that.

"I'm glad she's found someone who clearly loves her as much as she deserves," Mom whispers, wiping away tears.

"Okay, can we stop talking about me like I'm not in the room?"

Jack laughs, and Mom smiles. "Sorry, honey," she says. "Let's get dinner going, shall we?"

We go into the kitchen so Mom can finish preparing dinner. Jack insists on helping her, so I sit and watch, aware of how lucky I am to have the two of them. They chat away like old friends, as if they've known each other for years.

"This is delicious," Jack says when we sit down to eat. "You'll have to teach me to cook so I can impress your daughter."

I laugh and take a bite of lasagna, which I have to admit is pretty damn good.

"If you could learn to make this, I'd be very grateful," I say, hoping he catches the twinkle in my eye. He does and turns to Mom.

"Yes, I'm definitely going to need that recipe."

Right through dinner, the conversation flows. Not once does it feel awkward or forced. It's like Jack being here with us is the most natural thing in the world. After dinner, Jack insists on helping clean up too, while I go and get ready for our night out.

"I'll wash the dishes," I hear him say to Mom as I'm walking up the stairs.

"Are you sure you know how?" I call out.

"Watch it," he growls back.

I bite my lip and continue to my room, not nervous about leaving them alone at all. It's obvious they get along well and I love it.

After I'm showered, I do my makeup and hair, then I slip into the dress; a raw silk number that finishes above the knee and dips low at the back. It fits me perfectly, hugging my curves in all the right places. I smile at my reflection. My boobs look huge in this dress, which is something I'm sure Jack will appreciate. Slipping on some low heels, I grab my clutch and walk downstairs.

Mom and Jack are in the living room, talking. He stops mid-sentence when I appear and stares at me.

"Do I look okay?" I ask, butterflies dancing in my stomach.

He walks over and takes my hand. "You look more than okay. You're incredible."

"He's right," Mom agrees, her eyes wet. "Beautiful. You'll outshine every woman at the show."

"Mom." I roll my eyes, when Mom starts crying; it's a sign we need to leave and fast. "See you tomorrow," I say, kissing her on the cheek.

"It was lovely to meet you, Jill." Jack gives her a warm hug. "I'll take good care of her; I promise."

We walk out to the car, where Victor is waiting for us, the whole time Jack can't keep his hands off me. I turn to swat him away. He takes my hand and pulls me toward him for a kiss.

"Stop it," I hiss, laughing.

"No, I can't keep my hands off you," he murmurs. "I don't know if you know this, but I kind of think you're irresistible."

"Well, it's a good thing the feeling is mutual," I tease, giving him a quick peck on the lips, before walking over to the car.

On the drive to the club, I can feel Jack's gaze burning through me.

"Don't you know it's rude to stare," I tease.

"Then you should've worn something less sexy. Then again, you could be wearing anything, and I'd find you sexy." I smile at him, my heart racing. "Did I mention how good your boobs look in that dress?"

I laugh and shoot a look in Victor's direction, but his eyes are on the road.

"Behave," I say, snuggling against Jack.

I gaze out the window, a rush of emotion hitting me. The last few weeks have been like a dream. So much has happened and while it hasn't all been good, finding someone like Jack is something I'd almost given up on.

"You look lost in thought."

"I'm just thinking. Nothing bad, I promise," I add when I see his concern.

"What about?" he asks.

"Just how lucky I am," I admit.

"I'm the lucky one," he teases. "I have the most amazing girl a guy could ask for."

Disregarding Victor in the front, he leans close to me and kisses me on the lips. I moan softly into his mouth, my body tingling. We kiss again, and I have to stop myself from letting things go any further.

✦

We pull to a stop out the front of a stadium. I turn to Jack, confused, because this is not what I was expecting. When Jack said a show, I pictured an intimate lounge, with a few select people. Not a freaking stadium.

192

"I was expecting some little club."

Jack throws his head back and laughs. "God no. King's a big deal. Just ask him."

I giggle. King does strike me as the type to brag about his successes.

"Ready to go in?" he asks.

I nod. "Ready."

We go in via the side door, bypassing the massive line waiting to get through the front entrance. It takes me a second to realize we've entered right near the stage. I gawk at Jack. This is amazing. We have the best seats in the house.

"We get to stand here?" I gasp. "Do you go to all his shows?"

"Yes, and when I can," he answers both my questions.

I shake my head slowly. "I can't believe I didn't realize King was this big of a star."

"Hey now, you're going to make your boyfriend jealous with all this talk about other men," he murmurs, giving me a possessive kiss on the lips.

I smile and wrap my arms around his neck.

"Trust me, my boyfriend has nothing to worry about."

"Do you guys do anything other than make out?"

We look sideways to see Ace frowning at us. Piper stands behind him, looking cute in shimmery silver dress.

"Why, are you jealous?" Jack teases.

"Hell no," Ace snorts. "I'd much rather have the freedom to kiss anyone I want. Like your sister, for example." Jack's eyes narrow, and Ace puts his hands up in surrender. "I'm joking, jeez."

"Shh, he's starting," Piper hushes us, nodding on stage where King is about to perform.

With Jack's arms wrapped around me, I close my eyes and listen to King's smooth voice. I'm blown away by his talent. I knew he was going to be good, but not this good. His voice is absolutely incredible.

After the first song ends, the crowd erupts into applause, then everyone goes deadly quiet as the next song begins. Every time I think he's peaked, the next song is even better. I shake my head, amazed and in awe.

Piper catches my eye and smiles. "He's pretty amazing, right?"

"He's incredible," I murmur.

"The first time I heard him sing, I was speechless," she gushes. "Now I come to every show he does, just for another chance to hear that voice."

The way her face lights up when she talks about him makes me wonder, once again, if there's history between them. Over the next few songs, I sneak looks at Piper. Every single time, she's wearing the same, doe-eyed expression as she gazes at the stage. I swallow a laugh. She's lucky Jack hasn't noticed the way she's looking at King, or he'd have a fit. It's obvious she's crushing on him. At least, it is to *me*.

Maybe nothing has happened yet, but I'm pretty sure it isn't by Piper's choice.

When the band takes a break midway through the performance, Jack and Ace go to get us a drink, while Piper and I head to the bathroom.

"King's pretty amazing, hey?" I say in the bathroom as we touch up our makeup.

She gives me a dreamy smile, but then she stops, her eyes narrowing.

"God, you're as bad as my brother," she grumbles. "Nothing is going on."

"But you want something to happen, don't you?" I tease, nudging her.

"What? No way." But the flush creeping over her cheeks tells me otherwise.

"Why don't you tell him?" I ask.

"You mean, aside from the fact my brother would kill me?" she grumbles.

"Ah, so you *do* like him?" I grin as we walk back out.

"Yes, Fine. I like him." She turns around to face me, throwing her hands up in the air. "I like King," she growls. "I have a crush on my brother's best friend. Are you happy now?"

"I am."

We both whirl around to find King leaning against the wall, his eyes firmly on Piper.

I cover my mouth with my hand, trying to hold in my laughter, while poor Piper stares back at King, her wide eyes, filled with shock and embarrassment.

"Shit," she mutters. "I was just..."

"Admitting you have a crush on me?" He reaches into his pocket and pulls out a card, handing it to her. She takes it and looks at him, confused. "My room card. At the Four Seasons. Come meet me after the show."

King saunters off before she can reply, leaving a stunned Piper almost at the point of hyperventilating. She turns to me, her eyes pleading.

"What the hell am I going to do?" she whispers. "Jack will fucking kill me if I start something with King."

"Forget about Jack for a moment." I smile devilishly at her. "What do *you* want?"

⚜

Thank you so much for reading **Jack**. We hope you enjoyed Jack and Ellie's story.

If you did, we think you're going to love what happens between King and Piper in the next book in the **Vegas Kings series** – **King**.

For more information go to www.mckennajames.com

KING

ACE

Collections/Anthologies

Royally Loved (The Royal Romances box set)

Inherit Love (Inherit Love box set)

In Love with a Prince (paperback)

ABOUT THE AUTHOR

Mckenna James is the pen name for a collaborative writing duo who share an addiction to sweet tea and a love for billionaires.

Since they don't know enough devastatingly handsome men with boatloads of cash to spare, they decided to create some. They specialize in fairytales for today's world featuring modern princes and heroines who speak their minds and carve out happily ever afters on their own terms.